Bernie's Collectibles
~ Moridorno's Letter ~

Book One in a series

By Dan Yerigan

Contents

Prologue

Terni, Italy

Six months ago, Alfonse Ricci returned home from a short run, retrieved a razor blade from his collectibles room and sliced open the box UPS left on his porch. His old bottle blew a seal and caused water to dribble down his shirt during his last endurance hike. So just in time, his new Bisphenol-free, Triton Copolyester arrived. He felt excited for the coming weekend get away with his wife, Aria. A lake-view room awaited them at a Bed and Breakfast on Lake Piediluco, a short forty-minute drive from Terni. *Just two short days*, he thought, *to breathe forest-scented air.*

The couple checked in Friday evening. Saturday morning, they chatted with fellow guests during the multicourse breakfast. Alfonse talked less, so sipped tea and took impatient glances at Aria while she finished eating and visiting. At last, back in their room, Alfonse put on extra-thick wool socks under his perfectly laced hiking boots and filled his new bottle with cold water. Aria decided to pass on a morning hike and headed to their sun-lit deck with a book in one hand and a cup of coffee in the other. "You go have fun," she said.

"I'll be back in a couple hours, Aria. I'm taking my good camera."

"Alright, my love. I'll join you on your evening hike, I promise."

"I'm looking forward to it already. I should be back by one, but I'll text you if I take longer. Then let's walk down to Obeleto's for a late lunch, okay?"

"Sounds wonderful. I love their Caponata. Have a good hike, my dear."

"I will, my love. Enjoy your book."

They shared a lingered kiss.

At two, Alfonse had not come back, nor had he returned Aria's multiple voice messages. She checked her phone and saw two bars of service, yet her phone remained eerily silent. She hiked around the vicinity, then paced in the front parking lot until three, when she notified the police. An officer filed a report and conducted a small search of the area but found no trace of Alfonse. He explained the need to wait twenty-four hours before an official listing, but when he saw the damp checks and pale hue on Aria's face, said, "Here's my card. Contact me at first light. If he hasn't returned, we'll move that timeline up."

By Sunday night, after the use of a helicopter equipped with infrared tracking, two police dogs and dozens of volunteers, friends and family, no trace of Alfonse had been found. They determined his cell phone stopped communicating with the nearest tower on Saturday at 11:42 a.m. On Monday a lone search boat trolled the shoreline while dwindling numbers of devout family and friends looked once more down slopes and under shrubs.

Desperation settled in.

On Tuesday Aria returned to Terni with her sister, who had come to help. As they entered the house, Aria became overwhelmed to see her home ransacked. Her sister called the police and the rain of tears resumed.

Chapter 1

Huntington, West Virginia

Working in the loft of his converted farm silo, Bernie made two piles of snail mail on his office desk: important, and what looked like junk destined for the shredder. He opened an envelope from the important stack that most piqued his curiosity; from the attorney's office of Attuchi, Bordino, and Parletto, the associates who handled the recent sale of a rare figurine Bernie purchased at an estate sale in Charleston. He won the bidding war for a Chippendale cabinet that included a set of China and an assortment of glass figurines. One of the figurines turned out to be astronomically valuable. From the Brandt Glass Factory, allegedly one of only four produced in Germany during the late eighteen hundreds, and the only one known in existence. The figurine sold at auction for over eight hundred thousand dollars. Bernie felt like he hit the lottery.

His left eyebrow shot up as he deftly pulled out a single page letter on high grade paper and read,

From: Attuchi, Bordino, and Parletto, Associates at Law,
10 Via Umberto Olevano,
Pavia, Italy, Liguria Pavia 16123

To: Mr. Bernard Maynard, Bernie' Collectibles
1859 Junction Ave.
Huntington, W. Va. 25716-3739   USA
Dear Mr. Maynard,

I'm sure you recall our recent successful and lucrative business together. Our firm holds the great honor of extending our representation for the investor who purchased your Brandt figurine. Our client is impressed with your company's endeavors

and the sensational back story you uncovered about the unique treasure. I believe in your trade you call this provenance.

For this reason, we reach out to you for a similar task concerning the provenance of a historic document. Our law office proposes a contract be drawn between your antiquities company, DBA, Bernie's Collectibles, and our firm on behalf of our client, who requests to remain anonymous for personal reasons. His interest is to determine potential merits within the contents of a document dating from the sixteenth century.

We are at liberty to offer full monetary (U.S. dollars) compensation for your company's time, necessary travel, food and lodging, and any other associated costs related to your investigation. If you have an interest, please reply at your earliest convenience via email: rattuchiabal@siq.net

Sincerely,

Riccardo Attuchi, Esq., Senior Associate

Bernie sat back and read the letter again, then looked out a window at the cottonwood trees swaying in the breeze. He clicked on the reply button but changed his mind and called Lilly at his store.

She picked up on the second ring. "Hey Bernie."

"Hi, are you busy?"

"Nope, just out-front chatting with Shandra. We had a rush, and she buzzed for me to help up front. It's quiet again now, though. What's up?"

"Well, that's always a good thing, I mean the busy part. Hey, I just got a letter from the law firm representing the guy who bought the Brandt figurine."

A brief silence enveloped as Lilly took in what Bernie said, then asked with a serious tone, "Is there a problem with the sale?"

The store's front door opened, and a customer walked in. Shandra stepped around the counter to wait on him.

"No, it's not a bad thing," Bernie continued. "He wants to hire me, well, hire us to do research on a sixteenth century document. And, get this, they're offering any budget needed, including travel."

"Wow, that's generous. Where would we be going?"

"Not sure. Is your passport up to date?"

"It is. What's the subject matter of the document?"

"He didn't say, but something about merits within its content. I need to respond with an email if we're interested and get more details."

"I'm interested. Are you interested?" Lilly asked, unable to control the growing excitement in her tone.

"Well, that's why I'm calling, you're the better historical investigator, our head archivist. After all, you found the figurine's provenance and made me rich. So, it sounds like we're both in. I'll let the law firm know."

"Awesome," Lilly said as she began to hop in place. Then the logical side kicked in. She stood still and asked, "How are you and I going to be away from the store at the same time?"

"That's a good point, but the store's been looking consistently full again, thanks to you, and I've been considering elevating Shandra to manager. She's the first person I hired when I opened, so she has over two years' experience and acts mature for her young age."

"And she's smart as a whip. I could tell right away when she trained me on the cash register. I'm sure she'll say yes."

"Plus, we have Seth," Bernie added. "He's been wanting more hours, and I'll ask my dad to fill in as needed. He's retired and familiar with some of the old stuff, having grown up with it."

Lilly chuckled, said, "Your dad's a good guy."

"I'm going to reply yes, then?"

"Oh, heck yeah, let's go for it! Hey, by the way, Shandra and I are ordering pizza and cokes for lunch if you're available around noon, walk over to the store. We'll share."

"I would love some pizza with my favorite girls, and hey, don't tell Shandra about the promotion until I get there. See you in a while."

Bernie opened his laptop and typed:

Dear Mr. Attuchi,

Thank you for your letter and proposal. After conferring with my key archival investigator, we are indeed interested. But I have several questions before we agree.

Mainly, can you provide details about the document and what goals you expect us to achieve? What merits are we looking for? What's a proposed timeline for this research? Lastly, where might we expect to travel?

Thank you,

Bernie Maynard

Bernie googled the time zones between West Virginia and found Pavia six hours later than the eastern U.S., then pushed send. *They're probably done for the day,* he reasoned.

Bernie checked his email first thing the next morning and quickly opened Attuchi's reply, he read,

Mr. Maynard,

I am pleased with your interest in the proposal, and I can gladly answer your questions.

Our client recently inherited a letter written in 1582 by a catholic priest inscribed to another catholic priest which is alleged to have meaningful clues within its verse. Although minor attempts have been made, no one has proven these allegations. We request your company conduct an independent investigation.

If you discover clues we deem worthy, you and an associate may travel wherever that information leads. The duration of your investigation is dependent on the depth and breadth of what you find. Either party may withdraw from the contract at any time for

any reason with seventy-two hours' notice. If after a reasonable length of time you find nothing, you will receive a termination notice from us. I have attached a contract which provides the necessary details.

Should you and an associate accept our terms, please e-sign the contract with provisos and waivers. Once we have those back, you will receive an emailed copy of the document. We expect your investigation to begin no later than six weeks from your signed acceptance. This offer is valid for one week from this email's time stamp.

Kind regards,

Riccardo Attuchi, esq.

Bernie clicked open the two-page contract, reading what Riccardo mentioned, plus a few stipulations like confidentiality and ownership rights. The deal seemed golden, but Bernie felt nervous, so he picked up his phone and called Lilly. He relied on her knowledge and prior experience, with her Bachelor of Arts degree in History from Marshall University and four years at The Brooklyn Museum as an archivist and assistant curator. After Bernie's call, Lilly walked the two blocks to the silo in high gear, almost breaking into a run. After a brief discussion, they e-signed the contract. The following day, back in Bernie's office, Lilly sat low in the Swiss Moldoff chair, bringing back memories of her interview. The chair's springs, weakened from age, squeaked with every rearend adjustment. Bernie printed two copies of the translated letter and handed one to Lilly, who welded her eyes to the page and read,

To thee, Father Fionscetti ~

Aditya toils no longer,
Rest cometh upon lilac wind
Hued face soft plied lekythos oil
Wine and mirth pour from amphora

Let fettered past lie
In warm darkness
Encumbered reasons
We entomb for eternity?

Lore holds fast to Eliana
As she slumbers
Emancipating shadows
Cast in her bowels

Allied forever in all things holy on earth and those from heaven
Despachal Moridorno, 1582

Lilly finished reading, then watched Bernie's eyes move across the last couple lines. She cocked her head and said, "It reads more like a poem than a letter, and I see fodder for deeper meaning. What's your take on it?"

"Hmm. It is intriguing, but I better run through it a couple more times and let the fodder settle in, then I think I'll send a copy to my buddy, Sean. He's a history professor at Marshall University. I took several of his classes, and he quickly became my favorite teacher. He had just received his PHD, and I was an older student, so we're close in age. After classes we used to go out for beers and discuss random segments of history."

Lilly replied, "Obviously, you both have a passion for it. I can't wait to meet him, and sounds like a great idea sending the letter, but what about the confidentiality part in the contract?"

"I'll ask Sean to keep things on the down low. He's a good guy. Besides, there must be other electronic versions and pictures of this letter out in cyber land already. Attuchi must know that. I mean, he emailed it to me."

"That's true. The electronic genie's already out of the bottle."

Three days later, Bernie sat in his silo office drinking coffee and crunching numbers when the shrill beeb-beeb-beeb of a backhoe's alarm broke his concentration. He paused to look out the window at the busy landscapers. Months earlier, during a walk near his store, Bernie noticed a realtor's sign for a land development and told his parents. Using family inheritance invested wisely through the generations since the Rockefeller era, they bought the land and hired a contractor. Bernie's converted grain silo became the only surviving structure from the Fletcher Farm. The quarter section of land nurtured seventeen generations going back to the eighteen seventies, with crops, hogs, and chickens before time and the city's expansion swallowed it up. Conveniently near his store, Bernie's silo stood at the end of the cul-de sac on Fletcher Street, along with four new multi-plex office buildings, two on each side, with ample parking and fresh sod going in. *Getting close*, Bernie thought. His computer pinged his inbox with an email from Sean. He opened it and read,

Hey Bernie!

I found your top-secret letter fascinating. Let's start with Father Eufrasio Fionscetti, born in Pescara, Italy and lived during the eleventh century. He served at Saint Cecelia in Albi, France most of his life, records show he died in Albi in 1129. (I couldn't find any birth records.) When you do the math, Moridorno was born centuries later and is writing to a guy who died more than three hundred years earlier. That's weird!?! I'll let you pros figure out why anyone would do that.

But then, Despachal Moridorno was certainly a colorful character. He may have used the dates to make the letter stand out. Born in 1521 in Naples, he was an alleged genius who became a priest, with skills as a painter, sculptor, and poet. He created most of his Christocentric work in central Italy, but moved around to numerous parishes in Europe, western China, and Russia. The church tried to isolate him due to his unpopular beliefs. Much of his artwork and poetry remained unsigned, so we are left to speculate what works may have survived and which can be attributed to him. He created most of his work for utilitarian purposes to benefit all mankind.

Moridorno got into trouble with the church because his scientific beliefs clashed with church doctrine. He became

obsessed with true verses false prophets and wrote an unwelcome treatise that tested boundaries between heaven and hell. (Did you ever read any William Blake?) Moridorno allegedly strayed into the dark side, something to do with mythic and even demonic theories. Surprisingly, I came across recent articles in European tabloids about Moridorno's satanic ritual having ties to a hiker who went missing in Italy. So, coincidentally with your letter, Moridorno is getting a revival - got to love those tabloids!

Moridorno disappeared in 1585 somewhere in France while returning from Denmark. Records state he wandered into the forest to relieve himself but did not return to the small group of travelers. They suspected foul play, perhaps a robbery motivated murder, but apparently nothing much came of an investigation into the cause of his disappearance and presumed death.

It must have been scary back then for those with scientific minds to be paradoxically constrained by church doctrine to a point where your beliefs might get you killed. Church doctrine held a fine line for those who strayed into heresy back in the dark ages. While researching this, it reminded me of the struggles Pierre Teilhard de Chardin had during more contemporary times, exploring theology while straying into indoctrinated boundaries. It seems like sometimes we are still living in the dark ages. Sorry, I seem to have digressed! (Who me? lol)

Back to the poem. Aditya is a name with a Hindu origin, meaning sun. Hued face soft plied lekythos oil / Wine and mirth pour from amphora - these lines mention vessels or vases that traditionally held the named liquids. Not sure who Eliana is, other than ties to a Greek name that means God has answered.

Hope this helps! We need to go out for a beer and catch up, it's been a while!

Cheers!
Sean

Bernie sent off a thank you reply to Sean and forwarded the email to Lilly, then finished his office tasks and walked to his store.

"Hey Shandra, how's it going?" he asked, after strolling through the front door.

Shandra looked up from behind the sale's counter and smiled. "Great! Online sales are brisk today. I've been packing up a storm. We even sold the pig and hen salt and pepper shakers!"

"See?" Bernie replied as he joined her at the counter and gave her a fist bump. "I told you someone would buy them."

"That's why you're the boss. Here's my dollar."

"Just proves ugly is only a matter of opinion," Bernie quipped.

Near the front counter, they listened to Seth pitch the sale for a vintage Smith-Corona typewriter to a smiling greying customer, who said, "My dad used to have one like this, I think I'll take it."

Finding the store running smoothly, Bernie headed into the back room to check on Lilly.

"Hello, just me," he said as a warning, so she didn't drop something expensive.

Her face lit up when she saw him. "Hello," she replied, and put down a small lamp.

"Nice, huh?" Bernie asked.

"I love it. It would look good in my apartment."

"What's it worth to you?"

"Well, it's a Valiant Bronze with a tree branch design. I'd list it at two-fifty, but would you consider one-fifty?"

"What did I pay for it?"

"One thirty-five," Lilly replied with a smile and a wink.

"Small margin, but you have a deal. Hey, did you see my email from Sean about the poem?"

"I did."

"What'd you think?" Bernie asked.

"It sounds like our Moridorno Despachal was quite a character who made waves with the church," Lilly replied.

"That's for sure."

"And I read some of those tabloid articles."

"Kind of weird, right?" Bernie asked.

"I'll say," Lilly replied. "Especially the crazy demonic ties that make people disappear."

Bernie said, laughing a little, "Well, you know tabloids might exaggerate things a little."

"Yeah, just a little. At least Sean gave us new insight, like illogical variations in time. I'm keeping up with sorting and pricing, do you mind if I spend the rest of the afternoon doing research?"

"No, we need to start," Bernie replied. "Matter of fact, if you don't mind, I'll join you. We just need to keep track of hours, so we get paid by Attuchi."

"Of course."

They retrieved their laptops and headed into the break room.

At four p.m. they compared notes.

"I'll start," Lilly said. "I think the first stanza has Aditya stop working or straining, so this line might mean the sun should stop working?"

"Sounds cold, but good start," Bernie said encouragingly.

"Line two," Lilly said with a British accent. "Rest cometh upon lilac wind."

Bernie smiled and paraphrased, "You get a break when the wind smells good."

"Not sure that takes us anywhere," Lilly replied.

"I wonder why the question mark after eternity?" Bernie asked.

"Maybe questioning the length of time, like how long the reasons remain entombed?" Lilly suggested.

"That makes sense, but for what reasons?"

As they discussed the last stanza, ideas got hazy, with inuendo about bowels that spiraled into silliness and diarrhetic potty-humor, so the pair gave up and helped close the store.

That evening at her apartment, Lilly got comfy on her couch and flipped open her laptop. She loved solving riddles and discovering intricacies buried in the past, even though it meant working after hours without approval, but she planned not to tell

Bernie. After swallowing her last bite of a tuna sandwich, she snaked her body onto the floor, then tucked her legs yoga style and began to analyze each line.

Aditya toils no longer. *On one level it could mean the sun stops shining, but maybe deeper it means death?* She jotted down ideas in her notebook. Rest cometh upon lilac wind. *Maybe the air smells good and it's windy and then she rests? That still doesn't make any sense.* She moved on to the third line, Hued face soft plied lekythos oil. *Putting oil on a face, maybe?*

She opened the email from Sean and read it again. An idea struck her, *Could the oil have been used as a preservative?* She jotted it down.

Fourth line, wine and mirth pour from amphora. *Sounds like they are having a celebration.*

Continuing through the lines, she finished paraphrasing, then read back through her notes:

<u>Meanings</u>

Line   *1 - Aditya stops toiling, the sun goes out, darkness, death*
         2 - Lilac wind is good, to cover death, decay smells bad
         3 - Oil skin preservative
         4 - Drinking at a wake? Liquids = vessel name
         5 - Something historical held back
         6 - What's warm darkness mean? Death, Hades
         7 - Chained, Heavy, Held back reasons
         8 - Assume Eliana is entombed. Why is there a question?
           mark after eternity? So, not eternity? An oxymoron?
         9 - Poem is about Eliana "Lore" Sean says God answered
        10 - Slumbers = Death, Resting, Dreaming?
        11 - Emancipated, but in shadows? Redundant
        12 - Cast in her bowels, made from a mold? Belly, Core

No links or clues popped out, so Lilly opened Meta, then X, and poof, two hours later she felt like bedtime.

The next morning, Bernie drove to an auction in Charleston and sent Lilly a text to expect new antiques midafternoon. She found humor in his irony, calling antiques new. Shandra had the day off, so Lilly needed to help on the sales floor as needed and give Seth his breaks. *Darn,* she thought, *I wanted to carve out time for more poem research.*

By midafternoon, Lilly finished pricing her fourth tote full of small and midsized antiques when the bay door opened. Bernie pulled in and turned off the van's engine. He jumped out, said, "Hi Lilly, check this out," He slid open the van's side door and held out his hands, palms up.

"Ta-dah."

In the van stood an ornate chair, three full-looking totes and a rolled-up rug.

"I see three more full totes," Lilly said sarcastically.

"No, silly, the European chair from the early nineteenth century with possible provenance."

"It looks in good shape for its age," Lilly said. "What's the back story?"

"That it belonged to Napoleon Bonaparte. I know you're busy here pricing and researching the poem, but I'd like you to look into the chair's provenance."

"I'd love to. It's a beautiful piece, nice find."

Bernie carefully lifted the chair out of the van and set it down in front of Lilly. She admired the wood's rich brown luster as she ran a hand along the seat and backrest upholstered with plush red material embossed with gold patterns of ornate leaves and a harp. The carved wood arms sloped from the back and curled under at the hand rests with an intricate circular pattern like the spiral of a seashell worn smooth from decades of fondling fingers tracing the grooves.

"May I ask what you paid?" Lilly asked.

"I won the bid at sixteen hundred, but I think we can get thirty-nine if we, as in you, find provenance."

"Sounds like fun. I'll add it to my list."

"I knew you would. Any earth-shattering sales?"

"Nope, it's been quiet, I haven't been buzzed up front all day. Seth boxed up a few online items earlier. I made sure the UPS pick up sign is turned around in the front window. Hey, I heard Shandra lost the shaker set bet."

"Yep, she won't bet with me anymore."

"I can't say I blame her."

"Have you given any more thought to the poem?" Bernie asked.

"Yeah, you know I can't help myself," Lilly confessed. "I spent a little time during my break this morning, but nothing popped out at me except why would Moridorno write a letter to a long dead person? Did he have a time machine? Maybe that's what this is all about."

Bernie smiled at her imaginative speculation, said, "Many mysteries to solve, including time travel."

After work, Bernie took Lilly, Seth, and Shandra out for pizza and beer. Shandra invited her new boyfriend, Chuck, to join them. After downing a couple slices, Bernie broke the news about getting hired to research the Moridorno letter and for his plan to hire another employee. Nods of agreement rounded the table since an uptick in exposure occurred when local newspapers and online outlets ran detailed articles about the lucrative Brandt figurine sale.

"I think now's the right time," Shandra volunteered, "We rarely have time to play on our phones like when I first started."

Laughter broke out. Bernie responded, pointing at Shandra, "See, Shannie, that's what I like best about you, your brutal honesty."

"Is she going to get fired now?" Seth asked.

More laughter.

Everyone looked at Shandra, then at Bernie, who replied, "No, I never let the good ones go, besides, she's management now."

After the enjoyable evening, everyone shared goodbyes. Like a gentleman, Bernie walked Lilly to her car, but as he turned to leave, an awkward hesitation glued him in place like the tin man needing oil. Lilly sensed the magnetism, and for the first time she looked at Bernie as someone other than her boss. After sharing troubled expressions, the pair said good night and Bernie walked to his car with consternation instead of Lilly.

At her apartment, Lilly tried to get Bernie out of her head, so flipped open her laptop, checked email, opened a few apps, and got bored. She clicked on the tv, and channel surfed, settled on an episode of *Friends*, then got out her notebook. The romantic side of her wanted there to be more hidden in the poem. Her mouth opened slightly as she tapped her pen on her lower lip and immersed herself in thought. *Were Aditya and Eliana based on actual people? Supposing so, how did Aditya die?* She opened a browser and typed: *Aditya,* finding the name linked to Hindu roots and commonly used for a boy's name referring to the sun. She typed, *Eliana,* hit enter, then scanned the associated sites: *Eliana Tanker Fire in Mediterranean, Child Eliana Williams Still Missing, Bio-Clinical Trials Held at Eliana Care Center, Elfie, and Eliana Jewelry – Give Her a New Best Friend, The Eliana Folk Band - new album Daughter of the Sun, Eliana Vase on Display at the Museum of the Royal Tombs.*

Her eyebrows shot up as she clicked open the last site and read,

Museum of the Royal Tombs of Aigai, Vergina. See the tombs of Macedonian kings, including Philip II, father of Alexander the Great. Visit the new on-loan pottery exhibit, including the Centurion Lekythos, the Artesian Basin, and the Eliana Vase at the Museum of the Royal Tombs of Aigai (Vergina). A UNESCO World Heritage Site.

She opened a new browser and searched for articles or pictures of the Eliana vase but found nothing. She opened a map of the region and zoomed in on the Museum, finding the location north of Athens, in the small city of Vergina, near the northwest peninsula of the Aegean Sea. *Oh well*, she thought, *that's a bit of a stretch.* Feeling a bit discouraged, she went to bed.

Chapter 2

Silo Office

The next morning, Bernie wrapped up a phone conversation with Katy Andrews, his top candidate to fill the store's new position. She accepted his offer with training scheduled to begin Monday morning. Katy, a single, middle-aged mother with a strong retail background, seemed promising. Her youngest child landed a job out of state, making Katy an empty nester with too much time in a quiet house. Bernie heard the thumping of a low-flying helicopter and looked out a window, then up at the domed ceiling and followed its curvature. The silo housed a berth of forty feet with a spiral staircase in the center that rose to Bernie's loft office. On the main level, a kitchenette with a nineteen-forties white enameled metal shelving unit stood next to a small, but nicely stocked mahogany bar from the Monty Saloon, a novelty from an Antiquequest auction. Finishing the silo's circle, a small powder room and storage closet led back to the main door and central seating area.

Bernie craned his neck, but couldn't see the helicopter as the sound dissipated, so he got back to work and finished updating the ledger, checked his assets against liabilities, then almost skipped back to his store, and said a cheerful hello as he entered.

"You're sure in a good mood!" Shandra said from behind the front counter.

"I am," he replied. "It's a wonderful day!"

Seth chimed in from a back corner, "It is if you love dusting shelves."

Bernie told his sales team about Katy and explained his plan for her training, then walked into the back room, asking Lilly, "Hey, how are you?"

"I'm good," she replied, and returned a warm smile. "How about you?"

"I'm having a great day, thank you. I just offered the new position to Katy Andrews, and she accepted. She starts Monday."

"Hey, that's great. I'm looking forward to meeting her. What can I do to help?"

"I'll have you show her the magic you do back here and work with her up front at times."

"Sounds good."

Bernie asked, "So, have you come across any hidden treasures worth a ton of money today?"

"Not just yet, but I have plenty of opportunity," Lilly said dryly, motioning to the array of antiques in front of her and the rack of full totes nearby. "Perhaps you purchased more glass figurines lately?"

"Sadly, no," Bernie replied.

"I did a little research on the chair, though," Lilly said.

"And?"

"No confirmed links to Napoleon yet, but I'll find them."

"I'm sure you will."

The conversation turned to the letter. Lilly said, "I have a hunch, but I'm not sure it's even worth mentioning."

"Try me."

"Okay, I poked around and found a vase in Greece named The Eliana. The letter mentions vessels twice, and used her name, so I thought maybe that's a connection, but it's a big stretch."

"That's okay, I like it. At least it's something," Bernie replied, sounding interested. "In Greece, huh?"

"Yes, in Vergina, on loan at the Museum of the Royal Tombs. It's north of Athens in the former Macedonia region. Unfortunately, they didn't post any pictures of that specific vase on their website, so I called the museum this morning. It's six hours later there, so it worked out nicely after..."

"Yeah, yeah, what did they say?" Bernie interrupted.

"Hold your horses mister antsy pants," Lilly chastised, "The lady spoke the English no much good, so communication was limited."

Bernie smiled at her imitation.

Lilly continued, "But from what I gathered, a variety of vases are on loan from..." she checked her notes, "Ah, the Museo di Capodimonte in Naples, Italy, and I know what you're thinking, so I checked. There are five cathedrals in Naples."

Bernie gave Lilly a blank stare, he said, "I'm not..."

She prattled on, "So I checked online, and then called all five to see if they had a record of Despachal Moridorno or Eufrasio Fionscetti."

Bernie's facial expression turned to recognition and his left eyebrow shot up, said, "Smart girl. Did you find them?"

"Nothing. No record of either one of them having lived there."

"Okay, anything else?"

"Yes, back to the lady from the museum. She offered to walk down to the exhibit during her break and check for writing on the Eliana vase."

"Wow, that was kind of her, what did she find?"

"She called me back and said she saw words, but didn't know what language, but thought Italian, since that's where the vase came from."

A thoughtful silence ensued while Lilly looked at Bernie, waiting for his response. A smirk tickled his face.

"Well?" Lilly asked and shrugged her shoulders waiting for a response.

Bernie finally replied, held up a hand then pushed down a finger with each number, "First, Moridorno is from Italy. Second, Sean mentioned he did functional artwork. Third, maybe the writing on the vase is the lore in her bowels."

"Oh, I do like that last reference," Lilly said. "I should have thought of that."

Bernie nodded confidently as he pushed down his last finger, said, "Forth, let's go there and check it out."

"Go to Greece? Seriously, Bernie? On this vague assumption? It's probably just a coincidence."

"Well, we have three coincidences, so I'm pretty sure Attuchi will approve it."

"Do you mean it? Both of us?" she asked, excitement trilled her voice as she began to hop.

"If we get approval, I'll book our tickets," Bernie said, as he headed for his laptop, then added, "We'll plan for at least four weeks out to get everything lined up." The following day, with affirmation from Attuchi, Bernie booked their flights. Shandra's role as manager broadened to include scheduling and making deposits; Katy caught on to the store's routines, and Bernie's dad offered to help on the sales floor as needed. Bernie checked his notes for anything left to do, then questioned his decision to leave at all. A mental battle ensued: *Maybe I should cancel, but then, I've only had a few days off since I opened the store. If nothing else, it will be like a paid vacation with a pretty woman in Greece.* Case closed, or so he thought.

Two weeks later, sitting in his loft, Bernie heard a knock. After spiraling down the staircase, he opened the door to find a USPS woman requesting a signature for a registered letter. A stray dog wandered by and barked at them from the street near her parked van. The woman turned wearily at the potential threat and reached in her pocket for pepper spray.

"Hey!" Bernie yelled at the dog. "Go home!" The dog appeared nonchalant as it sniffed along the street's curved curb and headed back up toward the busy intersection.

"He must live around here," Bernie said, then looked at the envelope, but didn't recognize the return address from Rome, Italy, with a nondescript acronym, STA.

"Or it's a stray," the woman replied. "There's not much residential around here anymore."

Bernie nodded and signed the form. He returned to his desk, sliced open the envelope, and unfolded a single page that read,

From the office of Diocesan Chancery, Canon Law
Cardinal Pierre Beufort
712 Via Aurelia
Rome, Italy 6-00165

Dear Mr. Maynard,

My name is Cardinal Pierre Beufort, global representative for the Successors To Apostles, a sacerdotal branch who preserves the good name of the Catholic Church. I recently learned you were hired by the firm, Attuchi, Bordino, and Parletto, Associates at Law, from Pavia, Italy, to investigate a letter of antiquity.

Rest assured, the letter written by Despachal Moridorno has been thoroughly scrutinized by our church and others who found nothing of significance. Unfortunately, since its theft from the Vatican many years ago, unfounded rumors have cast a shadow on our glorious light. For the sanctity of our sacred past, our job is to stop any further publicity concerning this letter's contents and unfounded accusations one might find in tabloids and other rubbish-filled online media.

I can save you a lot of time, expense, and effort by extolling the letter's simplicity, a mere correspondence between brothers of cloth from times long ago. On behalf of our holy Catholic Church, I request you decline your services and grant us privacy. Allow this small piece of history to remain at rest.

In Christ's name,
Bishop Pierre Beufort
Serving our Lord as a watchful shepherd

Remember our Biblical heritage:
Genesis 42:16

Bernie looked online, then picked up his phone and called Lilly.

"Hey Bernie, what's up?"

"Well, I just got a bazaar letter from a Cardinal Beufort from the Diocesan Chancery about the Moridorno letter. He claims to have ties to the Vatican and wants us to tell Attuchi we decline doing research, and…"

"Wait, slow down, the Vatican knows we were hired by Attuchi? Bernie, maybe it's a joke. Do you think Sean might have sent it?"

"No, it came registered mail with a Rome post mark. It looks legit, although I can't find their website."

"See, I bet Sean sent it."

"No, I don't think so. This Beufort guy said it's their job to keep rumors from casting a shadow on their glorious light. And that's not all, he included the Bible verse, Genesis 42:16. I looked it up."

"Okay, and?"

"I have it right here, and I quote, send one of your number to get your brother; the rest of you will be kept in prison, so that your words may be tested to see if you are telling the truth. If you are not, then as surely as Pharaoh lives, you are spies!"

"Wow, Bernie, that does sound intimidating."

"I know, right?"

"What do you think we should we do?"

"Well, first, I'll call Sean right now to confirm he's not pulling off a good joke on us. If he's not, then I'll call Attuchi in the morning and ask a lot more questions."

The following morning in his silo office, Bernie ended the call with Attuchi and felt a cold draft. He got up and closed the window, his brow furrowed with worry about what he may be getting into, and more importantly, Lilly. He picked up his phone and called her at the store.

"Hey Bernie, were you able to reach him?"

"Yes, I just got off the phone and there's more to this letter than we thought."

"Oh?"

"Yeah, it's definitely not a joke. Turns out our wealthy client recently inherited the original letter from his brother." Bernie paused for effect, then said, "His brother is the missing hiker."

An uneasy silence ensued. "So, it's true," Lilly finally replied in a worried tone. Then her voice rose a note with each word as she asked, "Someone may have been killed because of the Moridorno letter?"

"Well, they're not sure, but the hiker has been officially pronounced dead even though they haven't found his body."

"Do they really suspect foul play or are the tabloids just making stuff up?"

"The police don't know for sure what happened. About seven months ago he literally vanished during a weekend getaway with his wife at a lakeside resort. They don't have kids, but he had a good life with no apparent reason to just walk away from it."

"Do they have any leads?"

"None. But there's an outside chance he took off and doesn't want to be found, like he had a secret lover, maybe, or he drowned and hasn't surfaced yet. But that's not all, their house got trashed while they were at the lake the same weekend he disappeared."

"Oh no, were they looking for the letter? Like the original?"

"Maybe, but they obviously didn't find it. Attuchi said other collectible items were determined missing, so it might have been a coincidental burglary."

"Bernie, do you think we should back out?"

Chapter 3

Rome, Italy

Seated in his office near the Vatican, Cardinal Beufort and his legal staff member, Scott Tubero, listened to their senior canonist brief them on active cases during their weekly meeting. A warm glow emanated from the fireplace.

The canonist cleared his throat, said, "The next case concerns the Moridorno letter. Attuchi and associates recently hired Bernard Maynard, owner of an antiquity's dealership called,

Bernie's Collectibles in the United States. Despite our registered letter of concern, our sources confirmed he and a female employee, Lilly Halpers, have flights booked to Thellosinki, Greece."

"Do we know why?" Beufort asked the canonist.

"We do not know yet. They may simply be going on holiday."

Attorney Tubero interjected, "I know we discussed this case briefly at last month's meeting, but I need a refresher."

Cardinal Beufort turned to Tubero and replied, "It's a sixteenth century correspondence between fathers Despachal Moridorno and Eufrasio Fionscetti. Moridorno wrote the letter to a long-deceased priest to gain attention, but it caused a scandal that rippled throughout our diocese. Supposedly, the letter shows evidence of heresy that nearly got Moridorno excommunicated. It's alleged he planted clues leading to physical evidence proving Lucifer's existence. The scandal stayed mostly within our holy walls and the problem became lost to time. But, in eighteen seventy, the letter was stolen from the Vatican library. We were betrayed from within. Its disappearance remained a mystery and a nonissue until recently when the letter resurfaced under private ownership of Alfonse Ricci, our deceased hiker, who purchased it from the black market and began conducting research. He contacted the press, and the tabloids got involved. Now, with his disappearance, they have spread rumors about Moridorno's devil worship as the cause for his disappearance. It all makes for good headlines while giving our church a black eye."

Tubero sat up in his chair, said, "What a mess. We made a small issue a big problem."

"We did."

"But I don't understand, there's no statute of limitations on stolen property, why didn't the church reclaim its property from Signor Ricci when the letter resurfaced?"

Cardinal Beufort replied, "Oh, we tried, it went to court, but the Vatican struggled to prove original ownership. The trial caused more bad publicity, so we let the case go."

"I can still file an injunction or gag order." Tubero suggested, although it would be challenging to prove just cause."

"I suppose we could try that route, but now it doesn't really matter in our modern digital world, every tabloid has it, we'd end up chasing our tails. The letter is out there in cyber-land, so we must stay true to our current goal to dissuade anyone from poking around in our past transgressions. But we can't have more debacles like we had with the hiker."

"I agree," Tubero said. "Such a shame. I never did hear, how exactly did he die?"

"Just a freak accident, really. Alfonse was taking pictures of Lake Piediluco in a secluded area. When our regent approached to...visit about the Moridorno letter, Alfonse became startled and slipped on a wet rock and hit his head. Then things were handled poorly. They should have made things appear as they were, just an accident."

"I agree. Are we fully sanitized?" Tubero asked.

"He won't be found, God rest his soul. No witnesses. The mess was scrubbed, and the authorities left open the chance Alfonse fell in the lake and drown or ran away seeking happiness with someone else."

Tubero asked, "So how do you suggest we proceed with Maynard and his assistant?"

The cardinal shook his head slightly in thought, said, "Keep track of their location and figure out what they're doing."

"I'll get a tracer on them," Tubero replied.

"Good. Let's move on to our next case," the cardinal said, turned to the canonist and asked him, "What's the latest report on Putnam and Horn?"

Chapter 4

Thessaloniki, Greece

After ten pampered hours in first class, Bernie and Lilly felt the jolt of the landing gear hit the runway. Bernie hefted their luggage from the overhead bin, trying not to clobber anyone in the process and made nervous eye contact with fellow passengers. The airport looked mostly deserted as they walked to the transportation area and waited with a few other travelers for the next shuttle bus to the rental depot. With their six-hour time change, local clocks read four-fifty a.m.

At the rental station, Bernie and Lilly encountered a slight delay because their car needed a last-minute adjustment. *Strange,* Bernie thought, *never had that happen before.* But within a half hour, they drove through quiet streets guided by the glow of an arrow on Bernie's map app. Glancing back often in the rear-view mirror, and seeing no constant headlights, Bernie sat back in his seat and relaxed a little.

"Anyone?" Lilly asked.

"Nope. So far, so good."

After a short drive, Bernie pulled into the Kronos Hotel. The groggy desk clerk confirmed their reservations and checked them in. The next morning, they found a sidewalk café near their hotel and ordered coffee and bagels.

"Did you get enough sleep?" Bernie asked Lilly, then chomped on a bagel.

"No!" she replied. "Quite frankly, I did not. The clocks here say nine, but my mind is telling me I should be in bed, having just got up to pee. But…" she smiled and put her arms up, looking around, "Here we are in the land of the Mesopotamians."

"I know, Alexander the Great may have had coffee and bagels right here at this very café," Bernie replied with a grin.

"No," Lilly said, pointing across the street. "I think he liked that café better." They laughed, finished breakfast, and headed for their car. As Bernie drove, Lilly helped navigate west toward Vergina and the Museum of Tombs.

The pair made good time on the A2 Roadway, then turned south on the Pros Kypseli highway. After crossing the Aliakmon River, they merged onto a smaller highway with less traffic, stopping in Maliki to get snacks and use a restroom. Back on the road, they slowed at times to admire hills dotted with fruit trees and quant farm bungalows. By late afternoon they reached Vergina with plenty of time to explore a few side streets.

The museum proved easy to find, although blended purposefully with the natural surroundings. They drove by slowly to admire the grass covered dome with a sloped entrance into the side of what looked like an ordinary hill. Bernie turned toward their hotel, about a mile away.

"It has four and a half stars," Bernie said as they pulled off the tree lined street and into the internal parking area of the two-story Hotel Aigon.

"I saw that on their website," Lilly replied.

They parked near the office and wheeled in their suitcases, clicking over the small cracks in the pavement. A middle-aged woman at the registration desk gave them a genuine smile exposing a large gap between her upper front teeth. She greeted them enthusiastically in Greek.

"Hi, ah, we speak English. I'm Bernie Maynard, this is Lilly Halpers. We have reservations?"

"Ah, the Americans, yes and welcome to the Aigon. My name is Sabah. I take good care for you," she replied, using the back of her throat to rattle her r's.

Relieved they could easily communicate, Bernie replied, "Yes, thank you." He cleared his throat, then pulled out his wallet.

Room keys in hand, they walked up the external steps to the balcony and found their rooms, dropped off luggage, then compared rooms: each with two single beds, a small table and chairs, the bathrooms had standard toilets and sinks, but the shower consisted of a three-inch raised basin with a thin curtain surround.

"That might take some getting used to," Lilly commented. They walked to the back of her room. Bernie pulled open the window curtains revealing French doors opening onto a back deck with stairs leading down to a pool. Sunlight shimmered off the water, empty lounge chairs stood ready.

"Wow!" Bernie said with surprise. "This looks way better than the pictures."

"Oh my gosh," Lilly replied, looking out at the oasis like setting. "I don't see anyone down there."

"Let's go for a swim."

Bernie arrived at the pool first. After rinsing off in the cinder block shower building, he walked down the steps into the shallow end. The water felt warm. *Like a giant hot tub,* he thought, and sat down at the three-meter mark. After a while, he glanced up looking for Lilly. Worry lines formed on his forehead. *What's taking her?*

A few minutes later, she walked down to the pool wearing a black bikini top with a white towel wrapped around her hips.

"How's the water?" she asked.

"A little on the warm side but feels okay," Bernie replied, trying to stop glancing at her shapely breasts, then added, "Looks like we have the place to ourselves."

"We sure do," she replied, looking around. "I'll rinse off, be right back." She disappeared into the shower building and emerged a few minutes later dabbing the towel on her face, then tossed the towel on a lounge chair. Bernie's eyes wandered up her legs to her hips, then her breasts and up to her face. She wore a mischievous grin as their eyes met.

She put her hands firmly on her hips and looked down, asked, "Like what you see?"

Bernie's face turned crimson. He quickly looked across the pool to avert his simmering eyes, then stammered, "Wow, I...you look..."

"Like I used to be on my college volleyball team? Yes, I was," Lilly replied, saving Bernie from making up a feeble excuse. She normally felt uncomfortable when men stared at her body, but with Bernie, she realized his gaze felt more like warm butter.

Lilly walked down the pool steps and sat down next to him.

Bernie said sarcastically, "And you're right, I just thought you… played volleyball."

"Uh-huh. Well thanks," Lilly replied, smiling shyly. "I played setter and middle blocker."

"I'll bet you were good."

An awkward lull set in, then Bernie asked, "So, have you noticed anyone strange?"

"No, not really, not in a suspicious way. You?"

"No."

"Do you really think they, whoever they are, would spend the resources on us because we're investigating an old letter?"

"Seems they spent the resources for the hiker," Bernie replied.

"Maybe he was onto something. Maybe we're not the first ones to look at this vase for clues," Lilly said with a hint of worry.

"It's just speculation until they find a body," Bernie said. "Plus, if we don't find any clues here, this whole trip will be a non-issue. So, let's just relax and enjoy the trip."

"You're right. Let's not over think things. But I'm over this bath water, I think I'll get out."

"Me, too."

An hour later, Bernie and Lilly stopped at the front desk for dinner advice. Sabah recommended a café just a short walk away. Getting seated near the front, they looked at paintings of Greek Gods adorning the walls and smaller, pastoral Frescos above the door arches. Their waitress stopped by and took their order. Hungry after their swim and having skipped lunch, the mouthwatering aromas of baked bread, sautéed onions, and sizzling meats made the wait difficult. The Fasolada soup arrived and tasted savory with white beans and vegetables in a tomato and olive oil broth seasoned with cumin and curry. Main dishes were served, and they dug in, reaching their forks across the table to share samples of each other's food.

"What time should we head to the museum tomorrow?" Lilly asked.

Bernie paused, holding up a finger while he finished chewing, swallowed, then replied, "Well, it opens at nine, so let's be up and ready by eight, maybe go out for a bite on the way. It stays open until six, so we'll have all day."

They shared a slice of baklava and Bernie left a generous tip. The sun cast orange hues as they strolled through the quiet streets of Vergina, meandering aimlessly in a wide loop on the way back to their hotel. Finding a tree lined park, they stopped and sat on a bench overlooking a small fountain with the statue of Achelous, father of the Sirens. A group of local children kicked around a soccer ball nearby, their yells and laughter wafted through the evening air.

Chapter 5

Museum of the Tombs

The next morning, Bernie and Lilly pulled into the museum parking lot shortly after nine. Finding only a few other parked cars, Bernie parked in an end spot near the front. He got out and looked back at the entrance. *No one followed, so far so good*, he reasoned and chuckled to himself at his paranoia.

After paying admission, the pair walked briskly to a large wall map with an introduction in various languages. They read,

Museum of the Royal Tombs of Aigai Vergina
The Greek archeologist M. Andronikos moved to Vergina and discovered this site reveling four tombs. Two were plundered, but the tombs of Phillip II and Alexander and Roxanna's son,

Alexander IV were discovered untouched in 1977. These burial
sites of the kings of Macedon are preserved here for all to enjoy.

"That's pretty cool," Bernie said enthusiastically, then looked
up at the map and pointed. "Let's start at the weaponry display,
then make our way down. I'll bet the vase will be in the Domestics
section, here."

"That makes sense," Lilly replied. They walked briskly down
the corridor past restrooms, a gift shop, and a small vending area
with tables and chairs, then looked through the weaponry exhibit
at life sized wax figures of Philip II and his son, Alexander dressed
for battle. The next exhibit featured utensils for washing and
preparing the dead for mummification, laid out ready for use next
to couches and chairs inlaid with gold and ivory. Clothing lay
folded ready for wear in the afterlife.

Bernie and Lilly slowly lost the battle to remain patient, so
uncharacteristically hastened through exhibits of sculpted ivory,
animal husbandry and ancient building practices, then nearly flew
past displays of bone fragments and ancient jewelry. Finally, they
entered the Domestics area and walked past fabrics, rudimentary
knives, and clay kitchen wares, then found the pottery displays.

Lilly stopped in front of the Eliana vase, said, "Bernie, over
here."

Approximately a foot tall and eight inches around at the
lower bulge, the centuries old vase appeared fired with tan hues
and a sandy texture. On the lower bulge, Bernie and Lilly stared at
the crude writing scratched with something about the size of a
toothpick. Bending over, their noses nearly touched the glass
enclosure, Bernie said dryly, "I think I see two names, Valdemar
and Ansel, but otherwise, it looks Greek to me."

"It's on loan from Italy, silly," Lilly replied without
acknowledging Bernie's attempted humor. "It's got to be Italian,
but the characters are so small and run together, makes it hard to
read."

Below the vase a small information plaque read: *Eliana Vase,*
Sixteenth Century, on loan from Museo di Capodimonte, artist

unknown. With photography prohibited, Lilly got out her notebook and jotted down the vase's inscription and museum's name.

"The writing on the vase is not very clear, I hope I have it right," she said.

Bernie peered over her shoulder comparing the writing, said, "That looks good enough for translation."

After taking a quick look at the other vases and cooking wares, they walked to the tombs.

The detailed frescos and tiling appeared well preserved, as if recently crafted. Lilly felt a flood of emotions standing in the footprints of mythic lives while she peered up at the abduction of Persephone by Pluto, painted with an artist's perspective centuries before the Roman Renaissance.

Bernie checked his phone: 11:48. *The morning ticked by quickly.*

Excited to translate the vase's inscriptions, and ready for a break, they headed for the lobby and vending machines. Finding a table, the pair munched on foreign nutrition bars and sipped from small straws tapped into boxed apple juice. Lilly got out her phone and notebook, then tapped the inscription into her translator app. Bernie leaned in as they read,

Meritorious is Valdemar
For whom Ansel sets course
With an appetite for <word not recognized>
Reflecting off the Danube
A warm respite my Obuda

"It reads kind of like another poem," Lilly said softly."

Bernie replied, "But I'm not seeing any references to the letter, just the two random names and a river."

"True, but this gives us something to work with," Lilly assured him. "Like the Danube?"

"Yeah, that might be a clue for another location, I suppose, but it's a shot in the dark."

"So was this trip," Lilly countered and wrote the translated inscription in her notebook. "I wish I brought my laptop."

"I doubt you'd get free service," Bernie replied.

"True. How about we go get some food, then do some research back at the hotel?"

"Sounds like a plan."

On their way out, they stopped in the gift store for souvenirs to take back as gifts for friends, relatives, and employees. Lilly bought books; Bernie got a variety of t-shirts with the tombstone entrances emblazoned on the fronts.

"I hope I got the sizes right."

They drove out near the main highway to a mom-and-pop looking fast-food place they spotted on their way into town. After getting gyros, chips, and cokes at the drive-through, they returned to Bernie's room. He turned the air conditioning up a notch, and the pair sat at the small round table and allowed Tzatziki sauce to flow freely. After a quick clean-up, they opened their laptops.

"How about you look into the poem since you have a knack for it, and I'll decipher what Csillagos means?" Bernie suggested.

"Sounds good," Lilly replied.

Bernie keyed in the word, Csillagos, and hit enter, then looked through the sites that popped up: a band on U-tube, *nope*, an investment firm, *nope*, the name of a hotel, *nope*. He opened a broad-spectrum translator app and hummed.

"What?" Lilly asked.

"I found something. The unrecognized word is Hungarian, meaning stars. So, what's a Hungarian word doing on an Italian vase in a Greek museum?"

"Good questions," Lilly replied. "Seems Ansel sets course for stars." Her voice trailed off, taken hostage by a new thought, she added, "Using them for navigation to travel to Hungary, maybe?"

"It's almost too obvious," Bernie replied. "I found that Valdemar means ruler, and Ansel means nobleman's follower."

Lilly surmised, "So, we have Meritorious is our ruler, Valdemar, and Ansel follows him to Hungary using the stars to navigate. But who or what is Obuda?"

"I'll check," Bernie volunteered and found a link. "Okay, this is interesting, Obuda was a city in Hungary that merged with Buda and Pest and became commonly known as Budapest. So, now we have a specific city in Hungary."

Lilly added, "A warm rest in Budapest along the Danube." Her serene expression became serious as she licked her thumb, then paged through her notebook, said, "Ah, here it is, the vase came from the Museo di Capodimonte, where is that?"

Bernie keyed the information into his laptop, said, "It's in Naples, and we know Despachal Moridorno is from Italy. It's a stretch, but he may have some tie to the Eliana vase."

"Maybe he made it."

Bernie nodded in agreement, said, "I suppose it's possible, Sean said he was into the arts. So, maybe we are onto something here."

"What should we do next?" Lilly asked, "Research Budapest websites?"

"Seems we are pointed in that direction."

"Okay," Lilly said. "How about I research Valdemar, and you take Ansel?"

"Sure, but let's not work here," Bernie said.

"Where do want to go, down to the lobby?" Lilly suggested.

"No, let's go to Budapest."

"Seriously, Bernie?" Lilly asked, unable to conceal her growing excitement. She stood up and began to hop, then paced and spoke quickly, her mind in high gear. "But we don't know what we're looking for. We don't have any specific reference points like we did with the vase. Where would we even begin to look?"

"As I recall you like to hang out in libraries."

"I do," Lilly replied. "I like the way a real book feels in my hand and to have the variety of so many books is so inviting and relaxing. The vellichor takes me back to my childhood where some days…"

Bernie had stopped listening and interrupted her with logistics. "Okay, so first, I'll make sure it's okay to be away from the store a bit longer, then get approval from Attuchi, change our flights and book rooms. I'm sorry, what were you saying?"

"Nothing, never mind, Bernie, this is going to be so cool. I can't thank you enough for letting me travel with you."

That evening, Bernie and Lilly enjoyed a windless calm while strolling from their hotel to the near-by Oikogen Restaurant. A host led them to an outdoor table where a young male waiter took their order. *Freedo*, his name tag read. After a short wait, their food arrived.

"Is there anything else for you I get?" Freedo asked.

Bernie glanced at Lilly who shook her head.

"I think we're all set, Freedo," Bernie replied.

Freedo extended his middle finger, then spun his round empty serving tray on it like a basketball, slapping the tray's side with his free hand. Local patrons at adjacent tables began to clap in tempo. Bernie and Lilly joined in. The waiter launched the spinning tray high in the air as he gracefully performed a pirouette, then caught the tray just as he came back around facing his surprised, but delighted guests.

He took a small bow and said, "Apolaysty, enjoy."

Applause rewarded the entertainment.

"I bet he makes good tips!" Bernie exclaimed.

Lilly nodded as she dug into her Kleftiko baked lamb in lemon garlic sauce with roasted potatoes. "Very talented," she replied, then pointed with her empty fork at Bernie's Keftethes pork meatballs with house baked pita bread, said, "That looks really good."

It was. Bernie pushed his empty plate back, but still had room for dessert. While they waited to share a slice of flaky Baklava, a young boy stopped near the front entrance, and sat on an upside-down plastic pail, then began running a ragged bow along the three strings of his lyra. The music added a perfect touch to the magical evening.

Bernie paid their bill, which of course included a generous tip. On their way out, he dropped an American fifty-dollar bill in the young lyra player's hat. The boy's face lit up when he saw the denomination. Lilly felt a warm rush from Bernie's generosity and glanced at him with a tender smile.

After walking in silence, Lilly said, "We didn't talk much about Hungary."

"No, we didn't, did we? Do you feel like taking another swim? We can talk in the pool."

"Sure, that sounds relaxing."

Several families lounged poolside while their kids splashed in the water. Two beach balls flew around, batted by gleeful youngsters. After a quick rinse-off, Bernie and Lilly stepped down the ladder into the pool's deep end and sat on the inner curb, legs dangled in the warm water. The chatted about the poem and questioned their wisdom to go to Hungary for no clear reason.

Lilly felt excited and willing to travel to Budapest, but voiced some reasonable options, "Maybe we should fly home and think about it. I mean, what about the warning? If we keep nosing around, maybe someone will actually start to follow us."

"I think we'll be fine," Bernie said, shaking his head. "Besides, I already called Attuchi this morning just to run it by him. He likes the connections, so funding's approved. Shandra says everything's going well at the store, and we're only gone three more days. I just got off the phone with my dad and he thinks we should go just for the experience, even if we don't find anything more. So, the pro column is pretty full."

"I guess you're right."

"I've been watching behind us every once in a while, and haven't seen anyone tailing us. Have you noticed anyone or anything unusual?"

"No," Lilly replied. "And I've been kind of watching, too."

Bernie said, "Okay, so in Budapest, let's start at the library and poke around for names and references. Then if nothing jumps out, let's carve out time to do a little site-seeing and call it a paid vacation, sound good?"

"Sounds fantastic!" Lilly replied, leaking excitement.

"Maybe we can even find some antique stores," Bernie added.

"Maybe we'll find another Brandt figurine," Lilly teased.

"Maybe we'll find all three!" Bernie replied as he looked in Lilly's eyes and explored their depth. A beach ball splashed down near them, interrupting the serene moment.

"Sesanome," a young boy called from mid-pool.

Lilly swam out, tossed the ball in the air and served it back like a volleyball.

"Efcharisto!" The boy yelled.

"No problemo," Lilly replied, not sure what the boy said.

They lounged in the pool for another hour talking about the poem, the museum, and Mesopotamian history. Comparing the wrinkled skin on their fingers, they got out, said good night, and returned to their rooms. Bernie changed their flights and booked four nights in Budapest.

Chapter 6

Athens, Greece

The next morning, after checking out, the pair stopped for the hotel's continental breakfast. Bernie surprised Lilly with an extended trip south to fly out of Athens, taking in historical sites along the way.

"I hope you won't mind. I added an extra day for site-seeing since we're here, we might as well. My dad suggested it."

Lilly's eyes lit up. "I think he's a genius."

Bernie added, "I won't put this little side excursion on Attuchi's tab."

Lilly stood up and hopped her little hop, then leaned in and gave Bernie a hug. "Thank you," she whispered close to his ear, then kissed his cheek. It felt like warm butter.

They finished eating, packed up the rental car and headed east toward Thessaloniki, then turned south on the A1 Roadway at Kleidi. Two and a half hours later, they pulled into the Battlefield of Thermopylae and walked around reading historical plaques about the Persian invasion. They stopped at The Akrogiali Café, an outdoor pizzeria along the Mediterranean. Boats shimmered in the distance as the breeze wafted off the sea. Bernie felt obligated to order the Medi pizza with lamb sausage, olives, and fresh basil. At their table, aggressive sea gulls squabbled and screeched near their table as Lilly tossed small morsels of crust.

Back on the road, the miles melted through the rear-view mirror, and they soon entered the outskirts of Athens. Lilly helped navigate to the Hillo Hotel on the eastern edge, in the community of Stavros. The hotel appeared new. The lobby's center held a large Grecian fountain of Ceto holding snake headed sea monsters under each arm with water spewing from their mouths. They checked in, found their rooms, then went out to eat. Sleep came early.

The next morning, after a quick bite, they jumped in the rental car and decided to stop first at the Temple of Olympian Zeus, then the Acropolis. After wandering around a while, the pair toured the Temple of Athena Nike and the Erechtheion Building. For lunch at the Paridosiako Café, they shared lemony chicken and hades potatoes. Next, they toured the Theatre of Dionysos, the Santuary of Askiepios, then stopped at the Theatre of Herodes Atticus and sat on an ancient white stone bench.

Lilly pondered, "If we were sitting here six hundred years ago, I wonder what play we'd be watching?"

"Probably a Dionysian drama or tragedy, but as you probably know, back then, you'd be left home, and I'd be here with my dudes."

"Oh, I'm fully aware of how you men tried to keep us out, but just look at us now, only six hundred years later and we can watch plays with you boys, and drink and smoke and vote and stuff."

Bernie shook his head and smiled at her sarcasm.

Having made a giant circle, they walked to the parking lot and found their car. Exhausted from walking all day, they returned to their hotel for the night.

Two days of driving and sightseeing made time go by faster than usual, Lilly thought, as she sat next to Bernie in the rental car heading for the airport. After clearing customs, they found their gate and sat down. Bernie peeled a banana and took a bite, conscientious of Lilly watching him eat.

"You're sure you don't want anything?"

Lilly shook her head. "I'm sure, thanks."

Forty-five minutes later, Lilly succumbed to the drone of the airplane engines and fell asleep. Bernie looked out the window at the carpet of clouds, thinking about Budapest and flight time. *In the air for almost ten hours,* he reasoned, *but gain an hour with the time change, puts us in Budapest at around eight p.m.* A pocket of turbulence shook the plane. Lilly stirred in her seat, then rested her head on Bernie's shoulder. He liked the lavender smell of her hair and fell asleep with his head resting on hers.

Chapter 7

Budapest, Hungary

Hours later, the plane shuddered and lurched heavily onto a runway in Budapest and taxied to the terminal. After deplaning and going through customs without a hitch, they walked to ground transportation and hired a taxi to the Danubius Hotel. Their wheeled suitcases followed obediently and clicked over the tracks of the automatic sliding glass doors. Bernie and Lilly joined a small queue line of guests waiting to check in. The immense lobby's tiled floor made a large circular pattern that flowed into the center. Faint piano music wafted from the attached Oasis Lounge. At check in, Bernie surprised Lilly with upgraded side-by-side rooms and a shared balcony overlooking the river. Already impressed with the size and grandeur of the hotel, Lilly ran her hand along the textured wallpaper in her room. *It's perfect.*

After freshening up, they returned to the Oasis and found a table near the piano. Bernie ordered a top shelf bourbon on the rocks, Lilly a gin and tonic. They cozied into their dimly lit booth and listened to the piano man play *Beautiful Dreamer*, as they sipped cocktails. At eleven, they stumbled to their respective rooms and stopped. With her key card in hand, Lilly said with slightly slurred speech, "Bernie, I really appreciate you taking me along with you on this trip...these trips. It's truly been... magical."

Bernie looked over the short distance at Lilly and gave her a warm smile and hesitated to collect his thoughts. Said, "It's been my pleasure." He dipped his head slightly in a small bow. "I..."

"Yes?" Lilly asked, followed by a few seconds of awkward silence, Bernie replied, "I like your insights."

"Thanks. You have good ones, too. Well, good night." She swiped her key card, the solid green blinked as she pushed down the door handle, glanced briefly at Bernie, her smile faded as she walked into her room.

Bernie swiped into his room, flopped backwards onto his bed, and put his hands to his face. "I like your insights?" he asked himself quietly.

The next morning at the hotel espresso shop, Bernie and Lilly sipped lattes and planned their day. Lilly tore off a small chunk of the cranberry-orange scone and stuffed it in her mouth, then glanced at the city map of bus routes Bernie had laid out on the table.

"We get on here about a block away," Bernie explained as he pointed. "Then we'll get off here at the Dozsa stop and spend the day exploring the Budapest City Park, just south of here, see?"

Lilly nodded and chewed, then asked, "You chose this park because you thought we'd find Valdemar and Ansel? I thought we were going to a library."

Bernie smiled warmly, then replied, "Well, we are looking for a needle in a giant Budapestian haystack. I have to admit, I would be beyond surprised if we came across any names or references to the poem. But these places looked like fun and close to our hotel, so viola, here we are, a little vacation. I thought we'd use tomorrow for a research day. Let's just take a day to do some site-seeing."

"Have I ever told you I like the way you think?"

"No, but I like to hear you say it."

The bus pulled up and they shuffled aboard. New faces of passengers flowed on and off during two stops. Bernie studied each face, looking for any hint they were being followed. At the third stop, Bernie and Lilly stepped off and walked through the park along the tree-lined sidewalk toward the museum. Large areas of open space and small ponds stretched into the forested distance, reminding Bernie of Central Park in New York, a haven amid a concrete jungle.

The Szepmuvszeta Museum loomed larger than expected, containing over one hundred thousand pieces of international art from all periods of European history. After nearly three hours of browsing and reading, they made their way to the exit and toured Vajdahunyad Castle, built in 1896 using Gothic, Renaissance, and Baroque architectural styles. Getting suggestions from the admissions attendant, they walked a short distance to the Nyereg Café for cheeseburgers.

After lunch, they strolled around the vast perimeter of the park, stopping at a giant sundial called the Time Wheel, where Bernie took a selfie, then sent it to most of their contacts with the text caption, *Having the time of our life!* Lilly bought snow cones from a street vendor, and a couple brain freezes later, they came across an amusement park where Bernie won a small stuffed giraffe by knocking over bowling pins. Then, after a tumultuous roller coaster ride, Lilly felt queasy and needed to sit down. As she tilted her head back on the bench's back rest, Bernie tucked the stuffed giraffe behind her head like a pillow.

"Feeling better?" he asked with concern.

"Yes, much, thanks. I used to be able to ride roller coasters all day long."

"It's hell getting old, huh?" Bernie asked, then added, "I'm ready to relax at the hotel's pool and maybe order pizza later. What do you think?"

"I'm ready."

Bernie and Lilly sat in the shallow end of the pool admiring the hotel's wide, ornate columns that tapered to a high domed ceiling; broad stroked faux frescos adorned the dark blue walls. Guests lounged poolside while youngsters splashed in the water. A father launched his young son over his shoulder near the deep end causing frenetic laughter.

"My legs feel like we walked a few miles today," Lilly said.

"We sure did. But what a great park."

"I'm impressed, but I'm sorry we didn't find Valdemar or Ansel."

"Oh yeah, I thought for sure we'd find something at the amusement park," Bernie replied sarcastically.

"What time are we going to a library tomorrow?" Lilly asked as they moved from the pool to a small hot tub.

"It opens at eight," Bernie replied. "I looked up the location, and it's only a few miles south. Oh, this feels nice."

"And all to ourselves," Lilly replied as they settled chin deep into the roiling hot water. Bernie noticed a raised scar on Lilly's lower inner arm. "What's that from?" he asked, running a finger along the four-inch section of raised skin.

"I got that in an ice-skating accident when I was ten," Lilly replied. "Two teenaged boys were racing and got out of control. They plowed into a group of us. I got knocked down and a skate blade sliced through my jacket into my arm. I had eight stitches, and remember crying, not only from pain, but seeing all the blood pooling on the ice. Another boy had a broken nose. It looked crooked, off to one side. He was crying more than me as blood gushed over his lips, and down off his chin. Then he choked on it and sprayed me with his blood when he coughed. I always felt nervous of ice-skating after that."

"Yikes, no kidding," Bernie replied, then turned his back toward Lilly and pointed over his shoulder. "I have a scar, too." He liked Lilly's soft touch on his back as she traced the disfigured skin lightly with her finger.

She said, "It's kind of shaped like Africa. What happened?"

Bernie explained, "It's from a burn when I was five, standing in line at a carnival with my parents waiting for cotton candy. A customer just bought a scalding hot coffee and got bumped. Most of it spilled down my back causing a second-degree burn. I couldn't lie on my back for two weeks. The whole experience sucked."

"We are both scarred people," Lilly said with a chuckle.

"I know I am. I didn't get my damn cotton candy!"

"You poor spoiled baby," Lilly cooed, then pushed Bernie out into the pool. On his hands and knees, he crept back toward Lilly like a crocodile, then wrapped his arms around her in a bear hug, lifted her off her seat, twisted around and splashed them both into the middle of the hot tub. They came up laughing, then sank back down and sat on the bottom of the pool with their heads just above the surface. Bernie, seeing no one near-by, kept his hands on her hips. Lilly lifted her shoulder length hair out of her face then draped her arms over Bernie's shoulders. Their faces inched closer until their lips met, then parted. Lilly drew closer and wrapped her legs around Bernie's waist. He cupped a hand under each butt cheek and pulled her close. Through their thin swimsuit fabric, she could feel him. Their kisses became passionate as Lilly slowly rocked her hips. Bernie's breathing heightened for several minutes, then he leaned his head heavily on her right shoulder. At that moment, Bernie confirmed he fell off the cliff of love, but worried about the risks of getting involved with such a great employee. *Don't screw up a good thing.* Absorbed in the warmth of the water, and still feeling a tingle, Lilly felt a kindling bond with the kind-hearted man. She asked him, "Want to have a sleep over in my room?"

He accepted.

On their way to breakfast the following morning, they stopped by the front desk to cancel Bernie's room. The young female clerk's mouth turned up a little as she assisted them, and glanced quickly at Lilly, then back to Bernie, then back to her screen.

"Reason for the move?" she asked Bernie.

"A change of heart."

Lilly blushed. The two women exchanged a knowing look.

Lilly held Bernie's hand on the way to a nearby restaurant for a light breakfast, then the couple walked to the bus stop where Bernie bought passes at a kiosk. Making their connections smoothly, they walked into the massive two-story library. Built with Slavic architecture, the structure took up an entire city block. The central lobby appeared cavernous, with two stories of wood trimmed shelves holding books commanding every inch of space, some accessed only by movable ladders that slid along rails. In the center hung an enormous chandelier. Two rows of public computers surrounded the centrally located circulation desk.

After a self-guided tour, Bernie and Lilly returned to the library's computer area. Sitting next to each other, they scanned the library's database for possible books using Valdemar, and Ansel in their search. The names produced a couple hits, but most articles were written in Hungarian.

"We're going to have to do some translating," Bernie whispered.

Next, they wandered around the stacks and picked out books, then found a table to themselves near one of the tall windows and settled in to read.

"Budapestians sure like their air conditioning," Lilly said quietly, slipping on her jacket, then resumed paging through the book, *Budapest Across the Ages.*

Bernie read about Greek mythology dating back to the twelfth century that included the name Valdemar, and how his name came to mean famous ruler.

By midmorning, several books lay scattered on the table, but no discerning clues were found in any of them.

Let's take a break," Bernie said, and wrote a note written in crude Hungarian: *Am return, leave books.* They strolled to the library coffee shop for lattes and muffins.

Feeling revived with caffeine, they returned to their table, Lilly picked up a book called *Greek Poetry - A Compilation Through Time.* She scanned down the list of chapters in the table of contents. Finding no immediate leads, she placed the book upside-down in the finished pile and opened a copied version of an old *Budapest Census.* She checked the table of contents, then began flipping through pages finding the years 1560 – 1600. Using her index finger as a guide, she traced the rows of names, then stopped. A rush of adrenaline swept through her as she read the name again to be sure, and said in a whisper, "Moridorno, Despachal." In the date column she read, *1578.* She inhaled deeply.

Bernie perked up when Lilly mumbled and asked quietly, "What'd you say?"

"I found Despachal Moridorno in the census."

Bernie's eyebrow shot up as he leaned over.

She pointed at the name, said, "He lived here in fifteen seventy-eight."

"Wow, Lilly, good find," Bernie said, struggling not to shout.

"It lists him as a priest at the Church of the Assumption."

Bernie nodded with a growing smile.

Lilly pointed toward the bottom of the page, said, "Look at the small writing here. He got accused of heresy while he lived here."

"Just like Sean mentioned," Bernie said. "He couldn't keep his mouth shut."

"Yep." Lilly paged ahead to the year 1579, scanning names with her finger, she found him again. "He lived here the next year, too. Looks like he behaved."

She paged back to make sure she didn't miss his name earlier, then jumped ahead to 1580, said, "He's listed here in fifteen eighty, with no remarks again. But I don't see him listed in 1581."

Bernie did the math, said, "So he lived here from fifteen seventy-eight to fifteen eighty while serving at the Church of Assumption."

"Let's see where that is," Lilly said, and picked up her phone. "Here we go, looks like the church is just across the Danube a few miles north of here."

Bernie glanced at the time, said, "It's only ten to eleven, we have a lot of the day left. Let's go now."

"Alright, but I need to use the bathroom first."

"Me, too."

They left the scattered books and wandered off together. Upon their return, they found the books stacked neatly on their table.

"Did you do that?" Lilly asked.

"No," Bernie replied as they looked around to see who may have straightened them.

"That's kind of creepy," Lilly said.

"Probably a library employee," Bernie replied, glancing around at a few patrons engrossed in books. Then Bernie saw a folded paper sticking out from one of the books. He pulled it out and read in crudely written English: *Those who search in darkness always stumble and fall.*

"It's time to go," Bernie said, and handed the note to Lilly.

She read it at a glance and replied, "It sure is."

They scrutinized every person on their way to the circulation desk to drop off their books, then walked briskly to the bus stop. Feeling violated, Bernie unfolded his map and figured out how to get to the church while Lilly stood guard.

Three connections later, mouths agape and necks craned, gawking at the tall spires atop the massive stonework of the Cathedral, Bernie read from his phone, "The Cathedral's eleventh century architecture originally held a Romanesque style, but transformations occurred throughout the years creating the Gothic look we see today."

"Interesting," Lilly said, as they walked up the stairs and into the grand lady.

Clusters of worshippers sat in pews and counted beads, some knelt in prayer. Two clergymen visited quietly with a young couple near the front altar.

Bernie and Lilly walked at a reverent pace, glancing around for possible leads. They stopped at an etched inscription on a side wall. Bernie used his phone to translate, then shared his screen with Lilly, she read,

A strong foundation
builds eternal trust
as we walk along
God's chosen path

In a whisper, Bernie asked, "Do you think it means anything?"

"Well, it's obviously meaningful in a Christian sense, but I don't see any names or references to our document verse or vase poem."

Bernie nodded as the pair wandered around the perimeter, but nothing else stood out, so they left the church and walked around the outside of the building.

In the back, the church property held a large cemetery sprawling to the left with a locked entrance gate, on the right, a spacious rose garden. The pair walked under a vine-shrouded trellis and followed the inlayed brick path past hearty rose bushes growing along both sides. Hundreds of blooms broadcast hues of red, pink, white, and yellow.

Lilly inhaled deeply through her nose and said, "It kind of smells like cotton candy."

They passed a priest pruning stems who stopped his work as they neared, said, "Jo reggelt, Isten legyen veled."

"Hello, good morning," Bernie replied.

"Ah, English. Yes, it's a beautiful day in God's kingdom. Peace be with you."

"Thank you, and with you," Lilly replied smiling as she carefully accepted a pink rose from the priest. "What a wonderful place," she mused.

"It is indeed part of God's paradise," the priest replied.

As the couple ventured down the path, they said hello to a young woman who walked by with a fancy camera hanging from a red strap around her neck. Bernie and Lilly eyed her cautiously and gave each other a knowing look, then briefly quickened their pace.

Bernie stopped at a faded white plaque, cracked and covered with lichen.

"Here's a translation sign," Bernie said, pointing at a modern sign in English that read: *Peer upon a rose as God's love*

"How cool," Lilly said. "The original plaque looks ancient."

"It's been there a while," Bernie replied.

Bernie took Lilly's hand as they walked deeper into the garden and discovered more plaques with sayings. They took turns reading the translations out loud to each other, "A white rose is pure and holy," then another down the path, "Passion lives within a red rose," and, "A yellow rose is wise and joyous."

It turned into a game. Lilly skipped ahead and pointed into the thick shrubbery, said, "Bernie, you should find peace and gratitude as you gaze upon a pink rose."

"I think that's the best one yet," Bernie replied as he caught up with her and gave her a hug. "Especially since the priest gave you one."

Lilly gave Bernie a kiss, then ran ahead to the next plaque and waited impatiently for him to catch up. She read, "A lavender rose provides God's wonder."

"Sure makes me wonder. I've never seen so many roses before. This place is so..."

"Enchanting." Lilly finished his sentence feeling enraptured with tranquility.

"Exactly," Bernie said, "But even better with you here."

Lilly felt like warm butter and leaned into him. He wrapped his arms around her and kissed her forehead, said, "You're my pink rose."

Near the garden's exit, they entered a common seating area with several benches encircling a small pond with a central rock island. A fountain trickled water down the moss-covered rocks. Glancing around, they found themselves alone except for a pod of Koi fish swimming slowly near the pond's surface displaying orange, white, and black mottled bodies.

"Looks like a good place to take a break," Bernie said. "I'm getting concerned we haven't found anything yet. Do you think we missed something?"

"No," Lilly replied, "We haven't seen any names or references yet, but there's still a little more to see on our way out."

"That's true, and I appreciate your optimism."

They sat down on one of the benches and listened to the water gurgle. Their peaceful interlude got interrupted when Bernie's cell phone chimed.

He looked at his screen and smiled, said to Lilly, "It's a text from Ralph, my old friend from Gunther Academy."

Lilly nodded as Bernie began tapping a reply. She noticed a box near the side of the pond and walked over, lifted the lid, and saw fish pellets with a scoop inside. She flung a load of pellets into the water and the tranquil surface turned into a turbulent mass of greedy fish. She laughed quietly and glanced over at Bernie who still had his face in his screen, his thumbs flying. She thought about calling him over to witness the frenzy, but then changed her mind and retrieved another scoop of food. Giving her toss a broader heave, some of the pellets landed on the small center rock island.

"Opps," she said, then, in her periphery, she noticed what looked like the back edge of another plaque that faced the other side of the island. She walked around and discovered another one, cracked, and covered in lichen. Near the sidewalk, she found the translation sign and read,

Tranquil like a rose
Ansel rests with Ursus
near our river's birth

She inhaled sharply, looking over at Bernie, trying to call his name, but her air got stuck. She began hopping, then finally screamed, "Bernie! Bernie!"

Startled, Bernie jumped up, nearly dropped his phone, and quickly ran to her and asked, "Are you hurt? What's going on?"

"You won't believe it," she replied, pointing to the island. Bernie immediately pieced things together. He spotted the old plaque on the island, then looked down and read the translation.

"Wow! You found Ansel!" Bernie shouted as his left eyebrow shot up. He gave her a quick side hug. "This is a direct link to the Moridorno letter."

"He led us here," Lilly stammered, sounding mesmerized. She retrieved her notebook and pen while Bernie snapped pictures of the original plaque and the translated sign.

The happy couple walked back to the bench and sat down to collect their thoughts and reflect on the new poem when the young woman with the camera interrupted them. She asked a question in what sounded like Hungarian.

"Ah, we're Americans," Lilly replied.

"Oh, hello," the photographer replied with a heavy accent. "My name is Yanelia Varga. I'm a reporter for Magyar Nemzet doing an article about this rose garden. May I ask you a few questions?"

Bernie and Lilly hesitated and gave each other a questioning look, then Bernie replied, "I guess that will be okay, but we prefer you don't use our names."

"Sure, that's fine. So, what brought you to our rose garden today?"

Bernie deferred to Lilly, who answered vaguely, "Curiosity mostly. We experienced the grandeur of the church, then found this beautiful garden. A priest gave me this pink rose." Lilly held the flower up.

"Very nice. What brings you to Budapest?"

"Sightseeing," Bernie replied. "Just tourists enjoying your Hungarian hospitality."

"What was your favorite part of the rose garden?"

Lilly looked at Bernie and smiled, said, "The little sayings on the plaques, but this whole place is magical."

"I agree, it is beautiful. May I snap a quick photo of you two?"

Bernie replied, "I don't mean to sound rude, but do you have any credentials?"

"Of course, no problem, I have my press badge here," the photographer replied as she dug in her purse, then pulled out a beat up plastic covered ID dangling from a stained lanyard. Bernie looked at the ID but couldn't read it. He glanced at Lilly, who shrugged and nodded.

"Okay," Bernie said.

The reporter took a few shots from different angles, and one with Lilly holding up her pink rose. Yanelia thanked them and left.

Lilly asked, "Do you think she's really a reporter?"

"Her ID badge looked like it had been to a lot of places. Plus, she didn't ask any specific questions. I think she's legit."

"Let's look online tomorrow and see if we find us," Lilly suggested.

They sat and listened to the murmur of water trickle into the pond. Lilly said, "I have to admit, when we came to Budapest, I didn't think we would find anything, and now this happens. It's like Moridorno gave us a tap on the shoulder."

Bernie added, "Or like he's leaving breadcrumbs and I'm Hansel, you're Gretel. But now I'm getting a little psyched-out about where this may lead...and why."

"I know, right?" Lilly replied, then glanced around with the feeling of being watched.

Bernie picked up on her concern, asked, "What do see?"

Lilly shook her head as if to clear it like an Etch a Sketch. "Nothing, just had a strange feeling." She paged through her notebook to their new poem, said, "I think the first line is just filler to make it fit in with the rose garden theme."

"I agree," Bernie replied, and leaned over to see her notes. He could smell her perfume. *Sweet and sensuous like vanilla and jasmine.* Regaining focus, he added, "And based on Father Moridorno's usual cryptologic style, I'd say the second line tells us Ansel is somehow linked to Ursus, possibly like a bear in one of Ptolemy's treatises from his quadripartite."

"Wow, Bern, I'm impressed, but not sure what you just said."

"See? I paid attention in art history class."

Lilly gave him a weak smile. Bernie noticed for the first time that one of Lilly's front teeth stuck out more than the others.

Lilly suggested, "Line three, near our river's birth must mean where the Danube starts?"

"What? Oh, yeah, it must. I'll check." Bernie got out his phone and began tapping. "Here we go." Bernie sat up as he read his screen, "The Danube is formed by two small streams, the Breg and the Brigach."

"Okay." Lilly jotted the names down.

Bernie continued, "And guess where the two streams are located?"

"Somewhere in northern Hungary?"

"Nope. The Danube's birthplace is Donaueschingen, Germany, or however you say that city's name. It's in southwestern Germany."

They slowly turned toward each other and smiled.

"I'll bet Attuchi, and his client will be happy with what we just found," Lilly said with raised eyebrows.

Bernie shook his head slightly as his grin faded, "Very true and I'm sure they'll gladly extend our trip, but how long can we be gone before the store's inventory gets too low?"

"Yeah, nobody's sorting totes for hours on end," Lilly replied with a touch of sarcasm, trying to lighten Bernie's buzz-killing mood.

Bernie added, "But no one's filling any, either."

Lilly said, "Donny's chin gin, or however you say that name, can't be too far from here."

"I guess I could check with the crew and my dad. Maybe add another three days. Shandra and Seth are holding down the store better than I expected. Shandra seems to be a natural leader. They haven't called or texted with any issues or questions."

"That's a good sign," Lilly said.

Bernie continued, "She said sales are good, but not exactly booming, so inventory should be okay for a while. You seem okay extending the trip, right?"

"Bernie, my dear, that is a silly question."

"Okay, well, it's the middle of the night on the east coast, so I'll check in later tonight when it's morning back home. Then I'll change our booking plans if everything's green-lighted with our Italian piggybank." Bernie checked the time, added, "It's one twenty-seven. I'm starving, are you hungry?"

"I am." Lilly smiled and modified her emphasis, "I'm hungary." Bernie groaned as they got up and said good-bye to the Koi and the special rock island.

Within walking distance and near their bus stop, they remembered seeing a row of fast-food kiosks and food trucks. After coming to a mutual decision, the pair ordered Gulyas Goulash with Langos fried bread. Finding a bistro table, they sat down. Bernie tore off a section of bread and used the slab like an eatable spoon. Catching on to the idea, Lilly did the same. Making short work of lunch and with ample time left in the day, they returned to the library.

Sitting at the library's computer screens, Bernie whispered, "Let's start with books relevant to Ptolemy's Ursus."

"Okay, you look into that, and I'll look into the Breg, Brigach, and Donaueschingen's history."

Two hours later, a dozen books lay scattered on the broad rectangular table, some left open to relevant pages, but Bernie and Lilly found no solid leads and gave up.

Later that evening, Bernie tipped up the wine bottle and poured the last drops after a delicious dinner at Fernando's Restaurant, then called his parents. Bryson and Chris were having coffee at home on their veranda.

"Everything's good here. Travel all you can when you're young," Bryson advised with typical fatherly advice, but felt genuinely impressed with their adventures, even a bit jealous.

Bernie pushed the speaker button, "Dad, I have you on speaker, say hello to Lilly."

"Hello Lilly, we hope you're having some fun even though you're with our son."

"Hi Mr. Maynard," Lilly replied chuckling. "No, your son has been nothing but a gentleman, and we're having fun exploring."

They chatted a while, then wrapped up the call.

"Yep, thanks! I'll let you know when we get to Germany," Bernie said, then pushed end.

As they walked back to the hotel, Lilly asked, "Father's always know best, don't they?"

"So it would seem," Bernie replied hesitantly, thinking back to his bumpy childhood experiences, then shared a few of his bad-boy stories with Lilly, including car theft and a near prison sentence.

Lilly said with genuine surprise, "I would not have guessed that about you. You seem so kind and levelheaded."

"Well, thank you. I guess a military school can squeeze the spoiled criminal out of any young wayward boy. My parents had good intentions, but they were always so busy chasing money and keeping up with their social calendars. My grandma Fran has always been my inspiration for me to become a better person. She's my rock, although I've worked my way back into good graces with my folks, too."

Lilly stopped and gave Bernie a heartfelt hug, said, "I need to meet your grandma, Fran."

"I'll make sure you do. She's going to love you as much as I do."

Lilly looked at Bernie with glistening eyes. "I love you, too."

Back at the hotel, Bernie stopped at the front desk to inquire about renting a private hot tub he had seen advertised. He booked hot tub suite five for that night, from nine to eleven, and as a surprise, ordered a bottle of red wine, a red rose, and a box of chocolates to be waiting for them in the hot tub suite.

Up in their room, Bernie called Attuchi and got approval for further travel. Next, he opened his laptop and changed their flights to Donaueschingen, then booked three nights at a centrally located hotel. Last, he sent an email to Shandra telling her to enjoy their extended freedom and lower inventory levels.

"Okay, done," Bernie announced. "Our flight leaves at ten-twenty the day after tomorrow, so we have one more day of site-seeing while we're here."

Deciding to hang out at the pool before hot tubbing, Lilly practiced a modicum of modesty to change into her bikini and used the bathroom for privacy. She came out wearing a thick white bath robe. As the couple left their room, Bernie playfully pulled open Lilly's robe and slowly moved his eyes down, then up her exposed bikini clad body, stopping at her face. She wore a smirk, and with raised questioning eyebrows, asked, "Like what you see?"

"Just making sure you're wearing appropriate swim attire," Bernie replied.

"Well, I better do a suit check on you," Lilly said, as she pulled out the sides of his robe and glanced down at his feet, then slowly moved her eyes up his legs, then stopped and asked, "What's this little bump here?" She brushed the back of her hand across his crotch and felt it jump. Bernie smiled at her playfulness as they stepped into each other's arms for a kiss that became instantly wet and sloppy. Their robes fell to the floor, her bikini top landed on a lamp.

"What about the hot tub?" Lilly mumbled through Bernie's lips.

"Later."

They didn't make it.

The next morning, Bernie woke up staring at a ripple pattern on the wall created by the rising sun streaming through a gap in the curtains. After a hot shower, they got dressed for the day. Stepping out of their room into the hall, they found a tray on the floor with a slightly wilted red rose and a box of melted chocolates.

"What's this?" Lilly asked, inquisitively, pointing at the tray.

"I hope the staff drank the wine," Bernie replied, chuckling, then added, "I ordered this for the hot tub room last night. They delivered it to our room this morning."

Lilly gave him a loving look and kissed him lightly on the cheek, then whispered,

"Thank you for being so romantic."

Bernie put the tray in their room, and they headed for the hotel's restaurant.

During breakfast they discussed plans to visit the botanical gardens and zoo, then headed for the bus stop. After a short ride, then a short walk, life-sized replicas of elephants, lions and pandas greeted them at the entrance. The place felt like a jungle, with trees shading the pathways lined by immense flora and fauna exhibits. The animals looked content in their spacious domiciles. After three hours of wandering and snacking at food vendors, they headed to the bus stop where Bernie said, "Time for your surprise."

Lilly peppered him with questions as they boarded. He sat with a wry smile and looked out the window pretending to ignore her barrage of questions.

They stepped off the bus on the fourth stop. Lilly looked around curiously at the modernized older downtown area with tightly packed brick and mortar boutique shops.

"Why are we here, Bernie? We're going to an antique store, right?" she asked, and began to punch him lightly in the arm like a boxer jabbing with a right, then a left. "Huh? Tell me!"

As they walked past store fronts, Bernie looked up intently at their signs until he stopped in front of Darius Antiques, and said, "You were right, here we are."

Lilly's face lit up and gave him a hug, "What a fun surprise, Bernie!"

He held the door open for her. Inside, old paintings hung on both walls. In the center stood rows of shelves filled with antiques. On the floor, larger items lined the outer walls.

They stopped to check out a knight's full ensemble of armor assembled on a mannequin standing in the corner. They waved hello to the proprietor, who asked a few questions. Bernie explained he didn't plan to purchase anything due to the customs hassle and shipping costs. However, a few small items tempted him, like an ornately beaded women's handheld purse with a delicate gold metal carry chain. Bernie looked at the price tag: 58,911 forints, which, after asking, turned out to be $195 U.S.

Next, they admired a gold pendant necklace with three small green emeralds set in a triangular shape. The tag showed 188,820 forints, or $625 U.S. Bernie asked questions about the armor. In broken English, the proprietor explained he possessed a letter proving the suit was worn by Hartmann Von Heldrugen, a thirteenth century grand master in the Order of the Teutonic Knights of St. Mary's. She wanted twelve thousand, U.S., plus custom's tax, shipping costs, and insurance."

"I'll have to think about it," Bernie told the owner. She handed him her business card as they left the store.

The afternoon included looking through three other antique stores along Falk Miksa Street. After making a giant loop and nearing their starting point, Lilly stopped in a t-shirt shop, while Bernie returned to the Darius Antique Store to visit more about the armor. His true motive was to buy the emerald necklace, and surprise Lilly with it that night. They came out of their respective stores about the same time. Lilly carried a plastic bag. Bernie smiled and waved with the jewelry stashed snuggly in a pocket.

At the Tengri Restaurant that evening, the atmosphere felt like an oasis. Miniature palm trees adorned the wallpaper. The waiter made a final pass and cleared their plates. Bernie ordered a slice of Dobos cake to share, then reached in his pocket and retrieved the emerald necklace, placing the pendant in front of Lilly, letting the delicate gold chain trail across the tabletop. Her eyes lit up.

"Bernie it's..." She choked up and brought her hands to her face, her eyes glistened.

Bernie walked behind her as she lifted her hair. He nestled the gold chain around her neck and latched the tiny hasp. He leaned in and kissed her cheek, then returned to his seat and admired the emeralds dancing off her skin.

"It's beautiful...thank you," Lilly said, dabbing her eyes with a napkin. "If I forget to tell you later, I had a really good time tonight." She paused, then added, "I have a confession to make. I stole that line from a movie."

Bernie replied with a wink and a smile, "Well, as a matter of fact, I, too, have a confession to make. I need to return that necklace, it's just a loaner."

Chapter 8

Donaueschingen, Germany

The airport hummed with activity the next morning. At customs, Bernie filled out the necessary paperwork for the necklace. After finding their gate with an on-time departure, they boarded smoothly for the ninety-minute flight. Clearing inbound customs in Donaueschingen, they walked to the transportation area for a shuttle to the Hotel Landsden.

Getting settled into room 428, Lilly looked over Bernie's shoulder as he searched online for a public library and nearby sightseeing options. She let out a yawn, covering her mouth, said, "Oh, my goodness. Excuse me."

The yawn became contagious as Bernie reached up to stretch his weary body. "I know, seems we've been going nonstop."

"Well, we have been, silly," Lilly quipped, then asked, "So are we sticking with our usual modus operandi?"

"Yeah, that seems to work. Let's see what we can dig up at the Donaueschingen Library."

Finding some energy reserves, the pair decided against the beckoning nap in lieu of beckoning hunger. They walked down to the hotel restaurant for brats and chips, causing heavy food comas and the pull to return to their room and watch movies. Bernie couldn't remember which one they started but woke up at around two a.m. and briefly stared at the light from the tv dance on the walls, the actors' voices sounded garbled and meaningless. He found the remote rendering quiet darkness and an instant portal back to dreamland.

Chapter 9

Rome, Italy

Wood crackled, popped, and hissed in the fireplace. Shooting embers sparked against the mesh screen protector as they attempted to escape from the heat. The flames cast an orange glow that illuminated Cardinal Beufort's face and formed a fluid shadow of his movements on the adjacent wall. He stopped pacing and leaned into the fire to warm his hands. On his desk, his laptop screen showed a smiling young couple. The online newspaper headline read: *American Tourists Enjoy Rose Garden.*

Cardinal Beufort turned to Attorney Tubero, and said, "There's a strong possibility they found something. Moridorno served at The Church of Assumption in Budapest."

Tubero replied, "Right, and our team examined everything they would have seen. The church has a couple inscribed biblical sayings on the walls. The cemetery is locked, so they couldn't get in there, but the rose garden has poems about...well, roses. We interviewed some of the clergy and a few tourists. The couple didn't stand out in anyone's mind, besides the reporter. I sent an email to the journalist with more questions, but I haven't heard back yet."

Cardinal Beufort replied, "Good, sounds like you've cast a good net for any ties back to the Moridorno letter." Beufort turned to his canonist, asked, "It's confirmed they left Budapest and traveled to Donaueschingen, Germany?"

"Yes, my lordship."

"Why there, I wonder?"

"We're unsure at this point, my lordship."

"See if Moridorno served there, or had ties to their church," Beufort said.

"Yes, my lordship."

Beufort turned to Tubero, and said, "Continue to have our regents monitor their activity. They haven't caused any negative publicity yet. Besides, I'm gaining a personal curiosity for what they might be following."

"That's not our goal, sir," Tubero said.

"I'm aware."

Chapter 10

Donaueschingen, Germany

The next morning, Bernie peeled back their hotel room curtain to reveal fog with a misty rain. He said to Lilly, "It's supposed to lift by ten."

They grabbed a bite to eat at the hotel coffee shop, then walked two blocks to the bus stop that took them to the Donaueschingen library. Arriving after one easy bus connection, they wandered the stacks and found a few books of interest, then settled in at a table near a window, their new command center.

After two hours of searching, Lilly said dejectedly, "I'm not finding any connections." She motioned to the copied census books scattered on the library table.

Bernie looked up from the book, *Donaueschingen City History, A Travel Through Time, Vol. I*, replied, "Well, let's keep looking for relationships and names. Remember, persistence pays off."

Lilly nodded and got back to work, tapping her pen on her lower lip as she checked her notes, then resumed paging through the census books.

Within the hour, Lilly sat up quickly and rapped lightly on the table next to Bernie. In a voice full of contained excitement, she whispered, "Ansel lived here in fourteen forty-nine."

"What? You found him?" Bernie almost shouted, then quickly put a hand up to his mouth and looked around. A few patrons glanced at him. He stepped over to Lilly and whispered in her ear, "You're amazing."

"Thanks to the invention of digital micro phish," Lilly replied, and opened a translation app, then paraphrased the new information. "His full name was Hugot Fredrick Ansel, a fabric weaver, age twenty-six in fourteen forty-nine."

Working as a team, they gathered information from each year, and pieced together Ansel's life. Lilly wrote in her notebook:

1450 married to Anna Korth
1452 deacon to the clergy
1454 member of the city council
1459 obtained 'master weaver' status
1471-1473 listed on sabbatical in France

"Interesting stuff," Bernie said. "Does this point us toward France?"

"So it would seem."

"Well, I'm pretty sure we can't take enough time off to scour the whole country. This needs to be narrowed down."

"But it would be romantic to tour all of France," Lilly countered in jest.

"Okay, sure. I'll ask Attuchi for funding that."

They stopped for lunch at the library's café, then returned to their command center with a few different titles, growing the stack of books on their table. Lilly opened one written in English called, *Southern Germany and All Its Splendor,* while Bernie paged through *Donaueschingen's City History, Vol II.*

In less than an hour, Bernie piped up, said, "Hey."

"What's up?" Lilly whispered and leaned over.

Bernie pointed at the page, then at the translation on his laptop. "It's an article about Grober Bar Cemetery, which translates to Great Bear Cemetery.

Reading over his shoulder, she whispered, "Well, I'll be...that's a possible clue, Bernie. You found a reference to Ursus. Maybe Ansel was buried there."

"It is possible. I'll check its website." After a few taps, Bernie said, "It's Donaueschingen's first catholic cemetery, named from the bible's book of Samuel. It's a private cemetery and a registered historical site dating back to thirteen-twenty-nine."

"Wow, that's ancient," Lilly said.

Bernie checked the time, said, "It's after four, so it's too late to go today. Their website doesn't list visiting hours or a contact number and there aren't any pictures. It's eleven miles west of here."

"Okay, let's go check it out tomorrow."

That night at The Bosporus Bar & Grill, Lilly reviewed her notes while Bernie searched websites on his laptop. They sampled local beers and shared a giant cheese and sausage stuffed pretzel.

"Find anything specific about sabbaticals in France?" Lilly asked.

"Yes." Bernie replied, "Ansel could have been at any number of churches in France. I found a dozen, so far."

"That's not too many," Lilly reasoned.

Bernie held up a hand, replied, "That's just two dozen that start with an A."

"Uh-oh, does that mean we're not going to France?" Lilly asked with a touch of sarcasm.

"No, babe, I'm the kind of guy who takes his dates to German cemeteries."

"Oh, that sounds creepy."

Bernie gave her a wink and replied, "Says the lady who likes to read obituaries."

They clinked their beer glasses and tipped them back. Bernie ordered another round.

The next morning, Bernie flopped his hand on the nightstand feeling for his phone. His head hurt and the alarm increased the pain.

"It's eight twenty," he choked out through a parched throat as he tapped Lilly on the arm. She stirred, then tossed back the covers and walked naked into the bathroom. Bernie hefted himself out of bed and walked to a window and peeled back the drapes revealing overcast skies, then said, "Hurry up, I have to pee."

They showered away some of the alcohol's retribution and got dressed. Bernie opened a window. A cold breeze swept in, so he quickly closed it.

"Weather app says sixty percent chance of rain today," Lilly said dubiously from the edge of their unmade bed.

Dawning sweaters and rain jackets, they headed out, but stopped briefly for coffee and muffins at the hotel coffee shop where Bernie figured out bus routes to get them close to the Great Bear Cemetery.

"Looks like we'll have to walk or take an Uber for the last mile or so," he said.

When they got out of the car at the cemetery's front entrance, Bernie felt a wave of apprehension. He closed their door, then watched the car drive away and disappear around a corner. *Maybe I should have rented a car.*

The cemetery encompassed multiple city blocks, with a sidewalk skirting the perimeter. A misty fog made everything damp and chilly, and the area seemed unusually quiet, but fitting.

A tinge of worry grew in Bernie's voice. "This isn't what I expected."

"What did you expect?" Lilly asked, picking up his concern.

"I'm not sure, but not this," Bernie replied, as he studied the dated homes across the street, many needed paint. Mature trees grew twisted above large weed choked yards making the area feel abandoned. A few cars puttered by with rubber-necked drivers, providing a modicum of relief for Bernie's sense of isolation. *At least there's some other people around.*

Surrounding the cemetery stood a ten-foot-tall iron fence entwined with multiple generations of ivy. Inside, rows of various sized grave markers could be seen among the well-kept trees and shrubs. A narrow road in a grid pattern weaved among the plots.

Tall, arched metal letters welded above the iron entrance gate read, *Lambs Taken From Our Flock.*

"That's from scripture," Bernie said.

"Uh-huh, from Samuel, I'll bet," Lilly replied.

They walked to the gate, made with two half-sections that swung open from the middle, a padlocked chain wrapped around its juncture.

Affixed to the gate, Bernie pointed out a small, rusted metal sign that read, *Keine Aufnahmefamilie nur nach Telefonischkeit +49-682.*

Bernie translated with his app and read his screen to Lilly, "No admittance family only by appointment." He snapped a picture, said, "I wish I knew we needed an appointment. They need to update their website."

"Hey, what's that?" Lilly asked, pointing to a small brick building built into the thick ivy-covered fence. They walked over to investigate.

"Must have been used for admittance at some point," Bernie said, as he examined a small window with remnants of stickers and old tape clinging stubbornly to the glass. He cupped his hands around his eyes and peered into the dimly lit room. A broken three-legged plastic chair lay uselessly in a corner, an intact chair stood in the center. A back door leading into the cemetery was closed. On the inner sill of the window Bernie noticed an ash tray half-full of white cigarette butts smeared with red lipstick. Footprints in the dusty floor led mostly from the back door to the chair, and to the ashtray. He tested the sliding window, it didn't budge.

"Locked," Bernie said convincingly.

Lilly's expression turned to concern. She asked, "What? Were you going to climb through if it opened?"

"No...well maybe," Bernie replied, smiling. "I'm not sure I'd fit."

Lilly slapped him lightly on his arm as they walked down the front sidewalk, glancing into the cemetery grounds, looking for someone who might let them in.

After a few minutes, they turned left along the cemetery's side perimeter, then left again along the back, passing a locked rear gate, much less ornate than the front. Bernie noticed fresh muddy tire tracks imprinted across the sidewalk. They stopped and peered through open spots in the heavily ivied fence, but the grounds remained as quiet as a graveyard. *Must have just missed the caretaker,* Bernie thought.

They turned left again and walked along the other side perimeter, heading back toward the front. Bernie stopped to examine a heavily rusted section of fence that looked askance.

Lilly asked, "What are doing?"

"I want to check something."

Bernie grabbed two of the vertical bars and pushed where the metal looked split along a failed seam. The section gave way easier than he expected. Vine stems broke and snapped loudly as dew rained down from the foliage. Almost falling through the gap, Bernie collected his balance and quickly pulled the broken section back into place. Dozens of interwoven ivy stems served as hinges that held the broken section up like a gate. He stepped back onto the sidewalk with a sheepish grin and swept water from his clothes.

"Bernie, what in God's name are you doing?"

The pair glanced around nervously to see if anyone noticed his vandalism. Lilly glanced across the street into dark windows and wondered who might be watching.

He bent over and shook the water from his hair, replied, "I didn't think I could do that so easy."

"Okay Hercules, let's go before someone calls the cops."

Taking nervous glances, they walked down the sidewalk at a brisk pace, turned left and made their way back to the front gate.

"Well, now what, mister master of destruction?" Lilly asked, then suggested, "Why don't we call for an Uber and try a different tactic, like make an appointment?"

Bernie screwed up his eyes mischievously, a wry smile migrated across his lips, said, "We're already here. Let's just go in through my little custom gate. Look there's hardly anyone around. Who's going to care? Just a quick look. I promise we won't dig anyone up even though you might like to."

Lilly put her hands firmly on her hips and replied sternly, "You should not go in there without permission, Bernie."

"Not me, we."

Lilly looked at him indignantly, said, "I'm not going in there and neither should you." She paused, then attempted to impart reason, "It's still early, let's walk around again and try and find someone to let us in."

"That's just it, no one's around, so who's going to know? Look, this is an ancient cemetery, available plots must have run out ages ago, which means their relatives are probably long dead. I doubt anyone's going to care if we take a respectful look around."

"Bernie no, you saw the muddy tracks in back. We'll find someone."

"I think they left. Let's just take a quick look," he persisted.

"That's another thing, this place is huge, it might take a while," she replied, imparting more reason. "And what if Ansel's not even in there?"

"That's it. That's what we'll say if someone asks, we're looking for the Ansel grave and we mean no harm and we found the gap in the fence, and..."

"No," Lilly interrupted, "Even though you're sounding strangely convincing. It's still a no."

At a standoff, Bernie relented, "Okay, let's do like you said and walk around again. Maybe we'll find someone to let us in."

With that, Lilly locked arms as the pair set off for another lap but found no one to help them. No new tracks appeared in the back. And after making their third left turn, the broken fence came into view. Bernie slowed as Lilly tugged on his arm to keep his momentum up. He stopped at the newly formed portal and unlocked his arm from hers.

"Bye," she said, shaking her head and continued down the sidewalk.

Bernie glanced up and down the street, then across at the houses. Seeing no one, and much to the chagrin of Lilly, who stopped to watch from a short distance, he slowly pushed open the section of the broken fence just wide enough to fit through.

Lilly gazed back nervously as Bernie motioned for her to follow.

"No," she replied with a hushed shout. "This is crazy!"

Bernie motioned again for her to join him. At another standoff, and against her better judgement, she walked back to the gap, turned sideways, and shimmied through.

Bernie jockeyed the section back in place, making the fence look whole again, and gave Lilly a confident smile. He grabbed her hand and guided her across a grassy section of graves and onto the narrow, paved road. Brushing the moisture from their jackets and lower pant legs, the nervous couple looked around.

"See, no problem," Bernie said in a whisper.

Lilly shot him a look of mild disappointment, but he felt her excitement. They briskly walked between the rows of gravestones and monuments, reading names and dates on the lichen and moss-covered stones. The pair soon established a system where Bernie read names on the right side, Lilly on the left. Just under midway through their search, Bernie came across the Ansel plot surrounded by a short, ornately decorated black metal fence enclosing four graves with headstones.

"Lilly, over here," Bernie called out.

Lilly walked quickly to his side, said, "You found him...and his family."

The plot held three graves with modest sized markers, and a fourth taller stone with, *ANSEL,* chiseled neatly near the top. On the lower section, they saw typical years of birth and death etched in the stone along with four lines of writing in German.

"Do you see the name in the epitaph?" Bernie asked, pointing at the tallest gravestone.

"I do." Lilly replied, smiling broadly, she began to hop and clap.

"The name is the only word I recognize," Bernie said. "We'll have to translate the rest." He retrieved his phone and snapped a couple pictures of the grave plot and a couple selfies with Lilly. Then, just for fun, he attached a photo in a text to his dad, who took German in college, then typed: *Having fun in Donaueschingen Great Bear Cemetery. Hope all is well with you and mom!* He added a happy emoji and pushed send, then loaded his translator ap and began keying in the words from Ansel's tomb stone.

"Hey, stoppen sie warten direct dort."

Bernie and Lilly turned suddenly. About thirty yards away, they saw an older woman wearing a dirty apron with her phone to an ear. She walked hastily in their direction with her other arm extended and her hand up in the international stop position. Bernie and Lilly looked at each other with raised eyebrows.

The woman yelled more words they didn't understand.

"Ah, time to go," Bernie said to Lilly.

"Just leaving!" Bernie shouted to the woman and waved, then grabbed Lilly's hand and they walked briskly in the opposite direction toward Bernie's impromptu gate.

"She didn't seem very happy to see us," Lilly said sarcastically as they turned right at the intersection.

"Stoppen Sie!"

Bernie glanced over his shoulder, said, "Good, she stopped following us."

The mist turned into a drizzle as they pulled on their jacket hoods and broke into a jog. Having been toward the center of the cemetery, the perimeter fence seemed farther than it should.

"We must be getting close," Lilly said, her breath short and peaked.

"Are we going the right way?" Bernie asked.

Faint sounds of a vehicle could be heard nearby. The pair gave each other a knowing look and broke into an all-out run as the drizzle turned to heavy rain and the wind kicked up. They came to another intersection.

"Right or left?" Bernie asked, panting, and disoriented in the sudden deluge.

Lilly looked left, then right, then left again, said, "Left...I think." They turned and ran full tilt. Finally, the perimeter came into view.

"There's our exit!" Bernie shouted through labored breaths.

A white compact police car pulled up behind them. Blue dots danced on the wet gravestones as Bernie and Lilly stopped and turned around. The car's headlights illuminated hundreds of fat rain drops splashing on the pavement. Bernie glanced at Lilly who wore a grimace. Small rivulets flowed down the folds in her jacket.

The car's front doors opened, and two police officers wearing rain gear emerged, one male from the passenger side, one female from the driver's side.

"Hechten, esht ahnsend specten," said the male officer. Bernie and Lilly glanced at each other, then back at the officers, and out of precaution, raised their hands.

"We speak English!" Bernie shouted over the din of the rain and whine of the windshield wipers.

The female officer motioned them over, asked, "British?"

"American," Lilly replied, sounding friendly and giving the officers her best fake smile.

"I am Officer Sneideker, and this is Officer Heiden. Do you have any weapons?"

"No, we're just tourists," Bernie replied, as they were patted down by the officers.

"I.D.'s, please?" The female officer asked. Bernie and Lilly got out their passports, soaking everything they exposed to the elements. Their backpacks were given a quick search, then stowed in the trunk.

The police officers got in their car and called in to headquarters while Bernie and Lilly were left standing in the rain.

"Let's just tell them the truth like we planned," Bernie said. Lilly agreed, but shook her head in dismay at their situation.

The officers held a brief conversation and eventually placed the young couple in the back seat of the car.

Officer Sneideker rotated slightly in her driver's seat and asked, "Why are you trespassing in this cemetery?"

Bernie pulled back his hood, ran a damp hand through his hair and replied, "We were visiting the Ansel graves."

"You are relatives?"

"No."

"This is a private cemetery. We were called by the caretaker who saw you snooping around the perimeter, then found you inside without a reservation. What reason have you to break in, causing damage to the fence?"

Lilly shot Bernie a sour look.

Bernie cleared his throat and replied, "This may sound odd, but we've been following names found in poetry, Ansel is one of the names. And, sorry about the fence. I can pay for the damage."

Officer Sneideker looked at first confused, then smiled and looked at her partner, saying something to him in German. He stifled a laugh, then with a grin, looked back at Bernie and Lilly.

"How did you get to the cemetery?" Officer Sneideker asked.

"We took a bus and then an Uber."

"Where are you staying?"

"At the Hotel Landsden."

The officers conversed in German, then the male officer picked up the radio transmitter and rattled off more German. Bernie recognized words like Uber and Landsden. A crackling reply from dispatch came back over the speaker.

The officers looked at each other briefly and shrugged, then Officer Sneideker rotated to face them again and said, "We are arresting you for trespass."

Bernie asked in protest, "We can't work this out?"

"Hold out your arms in front of you, please."

They were front cuffed and felt stuffed in the small car as they slowly drove along the inner cemetery roads. The caretaker slowly walked open the back gate and peered in as they drove out, her bright red lipstick highlighted the smirk lifting the corners of her lips, her eyes sparkled with laughter. During the ride to the police station, Bernie turned to Lilly and said in a whisper, "I'm so sorry."

Lilly, visibly upset, but not crying, replied in an emotional whisper, "You didn't force me to come with you. This is worth it...we both saw the name." Her frown turned into a small mischievous smile as she mouthed, "Fionscetti."

At the police station, officers frisked Bernie and Lilly more thoroughly, then confiscated their phones with enabled passwords. Next, the guilty couple were led to a windowless room with a square metal table and seated in two of the four solid metal chairs bolted to the floor. A camera with a small red light captured the room from an upper corner. Bernie bounced his right leg nervously and held Lilly's hand a bit too tightly as they whispered concerns.

"It can't be too serious, right?" Bernie asked rhetorically and formulated a plan to offer restitution. "I'll pay for the fence and pledge a generous donation to the cemetery, and maybe to the police fund."

After ten minutes of anxious waiting, two officers wearing suits entered the room and placed on the table two shallow baskets containing Bernie and Lilly's possessions, then leaned their damp backpacks against an adjacent wall.

"Hello, I'm commandant Fredricks, this is first investigator Heisenpf," the taller dark-haired officer said with a German accent. The four smiled politely and gave each other small nods as the detectives sat down across from Bernie and Lilly.

Fredricks continued, "So, I'll get right to the point. You have been detained for trespassing in a private sanctuary." He allowed a small pause and stroked his short-trimmed goatee, adding, "We have not officially charged you...yet." He paused again and glanced at his partner who nodded slightly.

"But we have some questions for you," Fredricks said.

Bernie stammered, still trying to be the epitome of politeness, "Yes, sure, of course. We already told the officers..."

"Yes, but we need more details," Heisenpf interrupted rudely.

Fredricks interjected, asking them politely, "Indeed we do, but before we get started, are you thirsty? Water? Coffee?"

Lilly shook her head slightly.

Bernie glanced at her response, thinking he could use a hot cup, but replied, "No, let's just get this cleared up."

"Okay, good. Let's do get this cleared up," Fredricks replied. "What is your business with the Ansel family grave plot?"

Bernie replied, "Okay here's the truth and it may sound odd, but we were hired to find clues in a letter written in fifteen eighty-two by a priest from Italy. Ansel is a name from one of the clues. That's why we were in the cemetery."

"My, that is quite an odd story," Fredricks replied.

"Sounds like bullshit to me," Heisenpf added.

Bernie motioned to the baskets on the table, said, "I think looking at the contents of our phones is bullshit! Is that even legal?"

The investigators gave each other a quick look, then Heisenpf replied indignantly, his voice grew loud and gruff, "Look, you are foreigners caught trespassing in a private cemetery after breaking a fence to gain entry." Spittle flew out of his mouth as he spoke. "We will investigate as needed."

Static-laced silence clung to the air in the room, then Fredricks said, playing the good cop, "What my colleague is trying to say here, is that we can never be too careful when we find strange circumstances."

"You two could be American spies snooping around where you should not be," Heisenpf said, pointing his stubby finger at them.

"Okay, okay, let's remain calm," Fredricks said.

Bernie and Lilly made eye contact in a knowing way when Heisenpf said the word, spies. Fredricks continued his good cop questioning, "So tell us about this letter and what you are looking to find."

Bernie replied earnestly, "Look, I'm just an antiques dealer, Lilly...Miss Halpers, is my assistant." He glanced at Lilly, then back at the investigators and continued, "We're investigating some names found in poems that led us here to Donaueschingen, to the cemetery and the Ansel plot."

Fredricks countered, "Yes, let's discuss that. Getting back to your possessions, we do have a right to investigate them since you were caught in the act of a crime, and we have examined your things here, your many photos, your assistant's interesting notes. You have been just recently to Greece and Hungary collecting these...poems."

Bernie replied, "That's correct, but I think you needed a search warrant to do that."

Fredricks asked, "Look, we've been through that. So, what are looking for, precisely?"

Bernie thought how to explain when Lilly blurted out, "We don't know what we're looking for."

Stunned by Lilly's outburst, no one said anything during an awkward moment. The investigators exchanged questioning looks, then Heisenpf raised his stubby finger again and pointed at Lilly.

He said, "Young lady, don't play games with us. We are not two stupid cops here, and you will tell us what you are looking for in our cemetery."

Bernie jumped in, "Okay, okay, here's what we know. In Greece we looked at an Italian vase at a museum which led us to Budapest, where we found information that led us here. It's the first time we did something stupid. Otherwise, we've been like typical tourists. I have receipts, I can prove..."

Heisenpf retorted sharply, a sneer distorted his mouth, "Typical tourists are not charged with trespass, breaking and entry, destruction of property, eluding police..."

"Eluding?" Bernie asked in protest, his voice rising.

Fredricks broke in, "Okay, okay, let's keep our heads here. Mr. Maynard, let's get back to why you were in our private cemetery. I ask you yet again, what are looking for?" Bernie glanced anxiously at Lilly, then looked intently back and forth at the two investigators and told them earnestly, "Look, all we have are names and locations that we find in poems. This all started with a letter from the sixteenth century. Honestly, we're not sure what any of this leads to."

They heard a knock at the door. Heisenpf got up and opened it slightly. A young woman handed him two printed sheets of paper and said something to him in German; he stepped out into the hall with her.

Fredricks got up to join them, telling Bernie and Lilly, "We'll be right back." The door clicked shut.

Five long minutes later, the investigators walked back in and took their seats.

Fredricks spoke first, "We have obtained your records, and it seems you are who you say you are, so that's a good start. However, our department has been contacted by a local representative from the Catholic Church. We have concern how they could know so quickly you were arrested here. Seems lately you caused them some trouble."

Bernie and Lilly exchanged a shocked look. The detectives easily picked up on it.

Fredricks continued, "He claims you are poking your noses where they don't belong."

"Like criminal trespass in a cemetery," Heisenpf interjected.

Fredricks continued, "Yes, like breaking and entering." He let these charges settle in, then offered them a deal to reduce them.

"So, if you agree to our terms, you will be released with no time spent in our lovely German jail facilities."

Bernie and Lilly nodded eagerly. "Sure, what are the terms?" Bernie asked.

"We'll reduce the trespass and other charges to unauthorized entry. In your country that's equivalent to a misdemeanor and carries a fine of seven hundred-fifty Euros. It won't complicate your ability to leave Germany, which is also a stipulation that you two leave the country within twenty-four hours. You will pay restitution for damage to the fence of twenty-five hundred Euros and civil fees of fifteen hundred Euros."

Bernie felt the sting of sticker shock with the fines. He stammered, "Okay, but our flights are booked for day after tomorrow."

Fredricks thought a moment, then said, "Alright, we can extend it to forty-eight hours, and don't miss your flight."

"Thank you," Bernie replied. "But about the church, may I ask who specifically contacted you?"

"That's privileged information," Heisenpf replied smugly.

"And it's against the law to investigate poetry?" Bernie asked flippantly.

Heisenpf stood up and caused his chair to tip back and crash loudly on the floor. He said, "I can't blame a church representative from protecting the sanctity of the dead."

Bernie stood up, too, said, "We were just..."

Fredricks stood up and broke in to deescalate the conversation, "Please, okay, let's just first sit back down."

Butts back in chairs, Bernie asked, "So, what's next? How do I pay? We'd like to get out of here."

"We accept plastic," Heisenpf said enthusiastically, as he pushed the baskets holding their possessions across the table.

Bernie opened his wallet and handed over his American Express card. For some reason, it took forty-five minutes to process the paperwork and fees totaling $4478.48 U.S.

Free at last and riding back to the Hotel Landsden in the back seat of their Uber, Bernie apologized to Lilly again for committing high crimes of espionage against Germany.

"It might be worth it, let's see what we have," Lilly said impatiently.

Bernie got out his phone and translated the verses from Ansel's tombstone as Lilly looked over to share his screen, they read as they sped along in the car,

> *Fionscetti weeps*
> *Where his lamb sleeps*
> *Vladimir forever endangered*
> *Our holy sanctity imperiled*

They sat quietly contemplating any meaning in the lines. Lilly retrieved her notebook and wrote them down, her penmanship tested by the car's bumps and jostles.

Whispering, Bernie said, "I think the first line gives us our reference to the letter and he's obviously sad."

"Right. I think line two references first Samuel, so we should look into that," Lilly suggested, then asked, "In line three, who is Vladimir and why is he in danger forever?"

"Maybe line four answers that," Bernie postured, then asked, "So what's imperiling holy sanctity?"

"All good questions," Lilly replied, then turned to look out her window and watched Donaueschingen whiz by.

Returning to the hotel, they quickly took off their damp clothes and hopped in the shower. Draped in each other's arms, the hot water rinsed away some of their anxiety.

They kissed. Lilly could sense Bernie's arousal and asked, "Sir, is that a weapon?"

"Yes mam, so be careful, it's loaded."

"I see that."

"Mam, you don't by chance have any weapons concealed anywhere, do you?"

"Do you need to frisk me, officer?" Lilly offered promiscuously.

"I think I better. Now, turn around and put your hands up against the wall."

Chapter 11

Rome, Italy

The fireplace remained still and cold. In the log rack, charred embers waited patiently for a little kindling and a match to entice a blazing resurrection.

"They were arrested in Germany?" Cardinal Beufort asked.

"Yes, they broke into a cemetery," attorney Tubero replied, "I emailed you the police report."

"I saw that, just haven't had a chance to open it yet."

"There's not much in the report, but they may have found something. The local authorities said they were following names and locations found in poems, and they were discovered looking primarily at the Ansel family plot."

"Do we know why?"

"We don't have all the details yet, but our local regent found the name Fionscetti on Ansel's tomb stone."

The Cardinal looked stunned and leaned heavily on his desk, then sat down, said, "My God, they are on the right track. We can't allow the press to link their arrest to the Moridorno letter. This all is beginning to stink again."

Tubero asked, "So what's our next move?"

"Have our regent give them a firm reason to stop meddling."

"I'll see to it."

Chapter 12

Donaueschingen, Germany

The next morning Bernie and Lilly sat at a bistro table in the hotel coffee shop sipping lattes and nibbling scones and wondering if their former day's experience had been a strange dream.

"Are you going to bill Attuchi for our arrest fines?"

"I definitely will, although I suppose they could dispute them," Bernie replied, as he searched websites for local attractions.

"Yeah, they may not pay for stupidity," Lilly said sarcastically, then picked up her notebook. She studied the freshly translated words from Ansel's gravestone.

"Why are you looking at that?" Bernie asked. "This is our last day here, so let's relax and have some fun. Even if you find a clue that says we should fly to Hawaii, I'm not changing our flights. We'll have plenty of time to figure things out when we get back home."

She looked up and met his eyes, then closed her notebook dramatically, asked, "So, what's on the agenda, Bern? Got any places lined up to break into?"

"You think you're funny," Bernie replied, then turned his attention back to his laptop and said, "Actually, there are interesting things to explore here."

"You mean without getting arrested?"

"Can we please stop with the sarcasm?"

"Okay, that was the last one, I'm done, I plead guilty," she teased with an accomplished smile.

Bernie shook his head, said, "There's a park about twenty miles south, looks like there's a visitor's center, some interpretive stuff where the Donaubach river joins and becomes the Danube."

"Sounds like fun," Lilly replied with genuine enthusiasm. "Let's go check it out."

Bernie smiled. *That's my girl, making a river's source sound exciting*. He continued, "So, we can look around there, then within walking distance, we can check out the Royal Fuerstenberg Collection of paintings, sculptures, and military paraphernalia, including, get this, Napoleon's travel urinal!"

"Oh, please, let's start with that," Lilly commented.

Bernie chuckled, then continued using a mock British accent, "There's also trophies, mineral stones, and other archeological wonders. Or there's the Museum of Art Plus, which has contemporary works, opened in '09?"

"Hmm, I'm not so much into contemporary art, unless you..."

"No, let's skip that one. Moving on, also close by is Jurgen Ruby Antiques!"

"Yay!" Lilly responded. "Let's definitely go there."

"There's another one called, Secondo Donaueschingen, a few miles west."

"Well, let's see how the day goes," Lilly reasoned and popped the last bite of scone into her mouth and zipped closed her backpack.

Bernie put his laptop away, tapped on his phone and ordered an Uber.

Forty minutes later and seventeen miles south, they wandered among the Donaubach, reading exhibits and displays. Stopping at the edge of a stream, they read,

East of here, the Danube River is formed geologically by the confluence of two streams: the Breg and Brigach. Hydrologically, the Danube's source is the Breg, the larger of the two formative streams located near Furtwangen.

After their self-guided tour, they walked over to the Royal Fuerstenberg Collection and wandered the three floors of the converted mansion, sharing a giggle when they came across the travel urinal.

Near noon with stomachs calling, they stopped at The Happy Deutschmann and ordered Jaeger Schnitzels.

"I enjoyed wandering through the museum and not have that feeling...that obligation to look for something," Lilly said reflectively as they found a vacant table on a nearby grassy knoll.

"That's true, seems more relaxing," Bernie mumbled through a thick slice of German sour dough bread sopped with creamy mushroom sauce.

Under the spell of a food coma, the pair waddled six blocks to Jurgen Ruby Antiques. As they walked in, three varying sized antique bells jingled in different pleasing tones as the door hit them. Bernie looked up. *I should get something like that for the store.*

The couple quickly felt absorbed into a world of wonder with a unique blend of well-aged wares spread before them. The proprietor smiled and nodded from behind the sales counter as he talked on his cell phone. Bernie and Lilly checked out the goods on their way up and down the many rows of shelves filled with old things. A half hour shot by like a bullet from a set of 1898 pearl handled dueling pistols, resting ying and yang in their worn velvet-lined case. Bernie would have bought the set on the spot except for all the export red tape.

After completing a casual stroll through the store, they enjoyed a lively discussion with the proprietor, Siger, a young man similar in age, who spoke good English and explained he had worked in the store since childhood. Lilly related her story, and they felt an immediate kinship. Siger had just recently taken full responsibility for the shop after the sad and unexpected death of his father.

"Siger Pulver is my full name. Nice to meet you and thanks for stopping into my modest store. Where are you two from?"

"Ah, Americans. Welcome, welcome. I would like to visit Virginia someday."

Bernie and Lilly said good-bye to the kind proprietor and the bells above the door chimed again as they left.

Bernie put Siger's business card in his pants pocket, said, "What a pleasant guy."

"He was, and we had similar childhood experiences. I should have asked him if his mother made up stories."

They chuckled as Bernie checked his phone for the time. He said, "What do you think, it's ten to four, do you want to go to that other antique store?"

"You said our flight leaves at seven tomorrow, right?"

"Seven – ten."

Lilly's expression turned to thought as she said, "So probably starts boarding at twenty to, half hour to the airport, through customs and security...I need to get up at...four-thirty. Yuck. I haven't had to get up early in a long time. You're spoiling me, Bern." She stepped into his open arms, said, "I'm tired. Let's just go back to the hotel." Bernie ordered an Uber.

Back in their room, they found a dead pigeon on their dresser stabbed in the chest with a small knife. Pinned to the knife a note with small rivulets of blood read: *Keep snooping and you may find everlasting peace.*

Bernie stammered, "Who would...why the hell...do you think Beufort, and that apostles' group did this?"

"Who else could it be, Bernie? That poor bird."

"In the name of Christ, they would go to this extent?"

Looking around their room, they saw drawers pulled out, a broken lamp, their clothes lay scattered on the floor.

"At least they didn't get our electronics," Bernie said, trying to sound positive.

"Or my notebook," Lilly whispered, her voice nearly breaking.

Bernie called the police first, then notified the front desk.

The police took pictures, dusted for prints, and asked a lot of questions, then bagged the bird, note and knife for forensics. The room showed no forced entry, so someone must have used a pirated scan key. The police planned to view surveillance cameras. Bernie and Lilly admitted their recent cemetery trespass, but omitted knowing any other reasons why someone would break in and leave such a threat. The police seemed skeptical and peppered them with questions looking for a deeper motive, but eventually gave up and left. The front service attendant moved the shaken couple to another room near the lobby and provided free valet laundry service.

Hoping to steady their nerves, they walked a couple blocks to The Klonenauber Pub and found a table in the outside beer garden.

"I didn't notice anyone following us," Bernie said with a hushed voice.

"Nor did I," Lilly replied. "But I need a beer, Bernie." She held out her hands. "Look, I'm still shaking. And think about that poor bird."

"I know, I know, how bizarre. This has to be related to that weird church office."

"I agree, this is bat-shit crazy for the Catholic Church to do something like this to us. They must know we're on to something."

Bernie said, "Maybe they know what we might find and don't want us to."

"It must be bad."

"Probably bad for them."

The waitress dropped off two beers.

Lilly said, "I'm really glad we're going home tomorrow."

"I'll drink to that," Bernie replied.

They clinked their glasses and drank deeply.

Chapter 13

Huntington, West Virginia

The familiarity of home felt warm and comforting, like a blanket woven from the green verdant hills. Bernie and Lilly eased back into work after adjusting to the time change and jet lag. Logistically and for safety reasons, they decided to stay at Bernie's condo. Lilly kept her apartment with three months left on her lease, but the couple rarely stayed there. They broke the news about their deepened relationship with friends, the crew at work, and both sets of parents. No one seemed surprised.

Bernie and Lilly looked over their shoulders a lot, a negative side effect induced by paranoia. For days, they entered the condo slowly, quietly, and peeked around corners half expecting to find their belongings in disarray. But no one jumped out of the shadows, and no dead birds appeared bloody and cold, their toiletries remained encapsulated. So, after a couple weeks, they started to relax again.

Bernie spent a few days at his silo's office updating the books, then attended sales and auctions to feed the inventory supply chain. He bought the knight's chain mail online from Darius Antiques in Budapest. Lilly got back into the groove of working at the store. In the back room, she popped in John Denver and pushed play on the eight-track player as she priced antiques. John's soothing voice flowed through the speakers. *You fill up my senses...* Lilly walked along the shelving rack and looked for interesting shapes through the plastic translucent sides of each tote box. She played a game to identify at least some of what each tote held, and it reminded her of impressionistic art, like back in New York, where definition languished in the fringes, and imagination filled in all the rest.

A hot pink sticky note on top of a tote caught her eye. In Bernie's handwriting, Lilly read, *Sort First*. Peering through the side, no impressionistic shapes stood out. She carried the tote to her workstation and unfolded the interlocking lid. Her eyes lit up as she peered down at over a dozen eight track tapes with an eclectic blend of styles. She lifted out a few, reading each label: *Anne Murray, Jimmy Buffet, Lynn Anderson, Peter Frampton*. A trove of fresh music genres. Lilly pulled John from the eight-track player and inserted *Peter*. She found a cardboard box and organized the tapes and realized they needed a proper retro tape case. *That's Bernie's next assignment*, she thought, excited to give him a big kiss for the new selections.

Chapter 14

Rome, Italy

A pungent pine scent wafted through Beufort's office from the stack of split logs waiting to burn. The canonist opened the next file on the modest stack, said, "There has been no activity to report with the Moridorno letter since Maynard and his assistant returned to the United States."

"Good. Our message must have been received," Attorney Tubero replied.

Cardinal Beufort smiled and sat up, said, "I'd like to think so, but these two are persistent. Finding a gravestone with the name, Fionscetti. That's more than a coincidence." He turned to the canonist, asked, "Any ties found with the other name?"

The canonist replied, "We're investigating the name, Vladimir, but as of yet, no ties have been determined."

Beufort addressed attorney Tubero and his canonist, "Continue surveillance and alert me if they book any flights. Let's move on to the next case."

Chapter 15

Huntington, West Virginia

The following week, Bernie's parents hosted a dinner party at their house and insisted he bring Lilly, since she had become more than just his assistant.

"Come and get it!" Bryson announced from his backyard patio. "Now, I made some burgers with cheese, some without." He put the platter on a table next to the potato salad, baked beans, sliced watermelon, and homemade rocky road brownies. A cooler full of iced beer and sodas stood open at the end of the buffet.

Lilly and Bernie were seated closest, but allowed others to go first, starting with Grandma Fran, who felt delighted to meet Lilly, then Bernie's sister, Rhonda and her husband, Glen, followed by a few friends and neighbors of Bernie's parents. Shandra, Seth and Katy were chatting with two neighbor kids near the pool. They sauntered over and got in line.

The food tasted excellent. Bryson licked his thumb and dabbed brownie crumbs off his plate and into his mouth like his father used to. After clean-up, the older folks sat around the pool chatting while the younger generation hung out in the pool.

Bryson announced some good news, "Last week we got a signed lease for the final office unit on Fletcher Street."

"That's great, dad, who's going in?" Bernie asked.

"A private CPA company."

"That's fantastic!"

"So, are you all packed and ready to play golf in Florida?" Lilly asked, aware of their pending trip.

"Not yet but getting close," Chris replied. "And thanks in advance for house sitting for us while we're gone. Lilly and Bernie gave each other a quick smile.

"No problem," Lilly replied, motioning to the water. "It comes with a pool."

Two weeks later, Bernie and Lilly sat in Bryson and Chris' living room watching Shark Tank on the sixty-inch curved tv. Lilly opened her pack, retrieved her notebook and laptop, then keyed in the senior Maynard's internet password.

"Going to do some poetry pondering?" Bernie asked.

"Uh-huh. It's time."

"Mind if I watch the rest of this?"

"Not at all."

He turned down the volume a few notches.

Since their return from Germany, the pair executed extensive research and held numerous animated discussions over a glass of wine but found only ambiguities and dead ends. Eventually, Ansel's tombstone poem lost its luster for Bernie, and he quit looking. Lilly didn't give up. Bernie looked on with admiration while his patient girlfriend searched for elusive clues. He billed Attuchi minimal hours and tried to sound optimistic when questioned about their apparent stagnation.

Lilly tore her eyes away from the tv and looked up a link to the Biblical verse in Matthew. *What God has joined together, let no man put asunder.* She keyed in sanctity, read, *Noun, the state of quality of being holy, sacred, or saintly.*

She stirred and sat up, hastily writing thoughts in her notebook.

Bernie sensed her shift in attitude, asked, "Find something?"

"Not sure. Probably not. I'm just kind of brainstorming."

"There's a shock." He sensed her concentration, so returned his attention to see if Barbara had made an offer yet.

Lilly looked up across the room staring, but not seeing, and asked herself, *why is Vladimir endangered, and sanctity imperiled?*

The bickering and bargaining on the tv seemed to grow louder and caught her attention. She asked, "Can we turn that down a notch, babe?"

Bernie complied.

Lilly fell back into her depths, *Okay Mr. Vladimir, who are you?* Tap-tap-tap. *The name is of Czech origin, meaning great peaceful ruler*. She scrolled past several articles about Vladimir Putin, then stopped and opened a site, *Vladimir is a city located on the Klyazma river, 200 kilometers to the east of Moscow*. She bounced her pen on her lower lip, then wrote in her notebook:

A person and a place.

Defeated great peaceful ruler or defeated city?

She picked up her laptop and opened a new browser, typed, *Was Vladimir Russia ever the site of a battle?* She opened a promising looking historical site and read, *A medieval capital of Russia dating back to the 12ᵗʰ century. Two of its Russian cathedrals, a monastery, and associated buildings have been designated as World Heritage Sites.* She sat up a little.

Shark Tank ended. Bernie turned off the tv and leaned over to see Lilly's screen, said, "You seem antsy."

Lilly asked, "Did you know Vladimir is not just a name, but also a place?"

"Hmm, I did not. But I'd wager it's in…Russia?"

"Yep, about two hundred kilometers east of Moscow."

"So, should I tell Attuchi we are traveling to Vladimir, Russia next?" Bernie asked with a strong dose of sarcasm.

"Now, hold your horses, we better think this through before you book any flights."

"I'm joking. Are you seriously willing to endure more threats pinned to dead birds? Or worse yet, we end up missing like the hiker."

"Maybe, but we don't need to become spies in Russia yet. I haven't found any conflicts in or near Vladimir to explain the last line, our holy sanctity imperiled."

"Good," Bernie replied. "I'm tired of traveling and looking for clues."

Lilly, engrossed in her laptop, said, "Me too, but only a little. So, the village of Vladimir started showing up on maps in the eleventh century with similar spellings."

"Hmm," Bernie responded halfheartedly, as he read an article in his dad's Golf Digest magazine on how to improve a drive by choosing the correct club.

Lilly nudged him, asked, "Hey, are you listening?"

Bernie sighed quietly and folded the magazine in his lap with a thumb stuck between the pages, said, "You have my undivided attention."

"That's better, now listen to this. I found trouble in our little town of Vladimir in the year twelve thirty-eight. Here, check this out."

Lilly handed Bernie her laptop, he read, *Vladimir was overrun in 1238 by Mongol-Tatars of the Golden Horde under Batu Khan. The grand prince's family perished in a church where they sought refuge, but the prince escaped. A month later he perished during the battle of the Sit River. After the Mongol invasion, the town struggled. From the years 1299 to 1325, Vladimir held the Seat of the Metropolitans of Kiev and All Rus. The See moved to the Kremlin in 1326.*

"Pretty cool history," Bernie replied. "Remind me what a See is?"

"Right, I just read that," Lilly replied, "It's Latin, from Sedes, meaning holy chair. The Holy See is the jurisdiction of the Catholic Church."

"Okay, so the Mongols invaded, but... what year did you say?" Bernie asked. "Overrun," Lilly corrected, "In twelve thirty-eight."

Bernie did the math, said, "From twelve thirty-eight to thirteen twenty-six, there's a gap of eighty-eight years before they moved the See, and it didn't seem like a big deal, right? The trouble began in twelve-thirty-eight. Maybe that's when the holy sanctity became imperiled."

"That's possible, but I feel like we're missing something. The dates are so close." Lilly countered.

"So, Russia's a definite maybe," Bernie said with a matter-of-fact tone. Lilly remained stoic, encumbered in thought.

They sat quietly for a while, then Bernie added soliloquiciously, "In one direction we have a possible link to Vladimir Russia, in another we have a link to France if we track down where Ansel lived during his sabbatical. Ambiguous clues that lead...where? Cryptic notes on impaled bloody pigeons...the missing hiker. Beufort and whoever or whatever he stands for is willing to kill because this letter leads to proof of Satan's existence? We must be missing something. Maybe it's time to throw in the towel and let Attuchi know we quit."

Lilly continued to ignore Bernie, then sat up quickly and tapped rapidly on her keyboard.

"What now?" Bernie asked. "Did you not just hear me?"

"I have an idea. What if there's a Vladimir in France?"

Bernie stood up and said, "Well, that's a good idea."

"Okay, here we go, there are profiles of Vladimir, a bunch of stuff on Putin, a French writer. But I'm not seeing a Vladimir, France."

Shortly after the senior Maynards returned from their trip to Florida, they invited Bernie and Lilly over for dinner.

"It will be just the four of us this time," Chris told her son over the phone. Then emphasized, "I didn't get enough one-on-one time with Lilly the last time."

The following Friday night, the four chatted pool side after dinner.

Bryson poured the last of Chris' favorite white grigio into the four glasses, said, "Thanks again for house sitting."

"Not a problem," Bernie replied. "We enjoyed lounging in the pool. "So, tell us about your trip."

"Yeah, how was Florida?" Lilly asked.

Chris perked up, said, "Well, like Bryson mentioned earlier, we didn't golf good, but the accommodations were nice. We had a great time with old friends and just got pampered."

Bryson added, "We only got out to the beach once, but at our age, we can't take the sun very long."

"And I can't walk through that thick sand very good anymore," Chris added.

The phones came out to share photos of Florida as the conversation veered to Bernie and Lilly's trip. Bryson had a question for them about the text Bernie sent with the photo of

Ansel's tombstone. Bryson brushed a finger over his screen. Bernie already found the photo on his phone and enlarged the picture. Lilly leaned in to see.

Bryson said, "Ah, here it is." Chris leaned in to share his screen.

"Yeah, what about it?" Bernie asked.

"Well, if you zoom in and look under the dates of his life, and just above the epitaph, you can see two very small numbers mostly covered by lichen. I was just curious about what those were for. Looks like a seventeen, then a space, then a seventy-eight."

"Oh, yeah. I see them now," Lilly replied with genuine surprise.

Bernie added, "Wow, I can't believe we missed that. Good catch, dad!"

Bryson smiled, said, "See? I still have sharp eyes for an old man."

Chris chimed in, "Actually, we were mirroring photos from his phone onto the big screen when he noticed them, so he cheated."

Everyone chuckled, Bryson added, "That's true. I looked on the computer but couldn't find any cultural common practice for putting numbers on tomb stones besides the obvious need for dates."

"I doubt it's a date," Bernie said, "Seventeen seventy-eight would have been more than two hundred years in the future after Hugot Ansel was buried."

"Besides, there's a space between the seventeen and the seventy-eight. I wonder why?" Lilly asked.

"Well, while you all solve the mystery, I'm going to go slice the chocolate cake," Chris said, getting up.

"Need some help?" Lilly asked.

"I would love some help, Lilly, thank you."

The women gathered plates and walked in the backdoor chatting. Soon cake and clean forks were passed around and the couples resumed trading stories about their respective trips.

Bernie broke the news about their arrest at the graveyard and hotel room break-in, including the dead bird.

A nervous silence settled over the table. Bryson exchanged a concerned look with his wife. He sorted a bite of cheesecake with his teeth, swallowed hard, then glared at his son, asked, "You still got in you, don't you, Bernie?"

The dimming light cast inky reflections of their turbulent past.

Bernie returned his father's glare, said, "Look, I didn't think it would be that big of a deal and I do realize that it wasn't the best decision."

"Does Lilly know about your past, Bernie?" Bryson asked, pointing his fork at his son while taking small glances at Lilly.

Bernie opened his mouth to answer, but Lilly cut him off, she said, "Yes, he's told me some of it, and I would never have guessed. You have a terrific son. All I see, all I've known, is the older, mature version...at least most of the time."

Bryson put down his fork and sat back in his chair. Chris sprouted a grin.

Lilly added, "I knew better and didn't stop him from going into that cemetery. In fact, I went in with him. Curiosity got the best of both of us."

The tension subsided. Chris excused herself, walked into the house and came back out with a deck of cards. After two games of rummy, the couples said their good-byes. During the drive home, Bernie and Lilly discussed the tombstone numbers, but the conversation turned silly.

"Maybe they are the combination to a time machine," Lilly pondered.

"Maybe they were Ansel's favorite lotto numbers," Bernie suggested.

"Maybe they hit the daily double!"

The next morning, in the back room of the store, Bernie helped Lilly sort and price items. Johnny Cash's *Folsom Prison Blues* blared from the speakers.

"Thanks again for the new selection of tapes," Lilly said.

"My pleasure."

"You know, I picked this song out for you," Lilly added with a wry smile.

Bernie looked up to concentrate on the music, then returned her smile, said, "Oh, I get it. Folsom Prison, right? You are a funny woman. But I didn't shoot a man in Reno."

"Just to watch him die? That doesn't sound like you. I'm glad no one got shot at the cemetery."

"Shot by the lipstick lady?" Bernie asked, then changed the subject. "Do you have any more thoughts on the numbers my dad noticed?"

"You mean serious ideas or jokes?"

"Either I guess."

"Well, you know me," Lilly replied. "I do have a serious one. Maybe the numbers might be used for tracking. Like how the cemetery assigned numbers to grave plots."

"Well, that's a possibility, but my dad checked into that, remember?" Bernie replied, then opened his photos and zoomed in on Ansel family's tomb stones. "Plus, no other tombstones in the Ansel plot have any extra numbers that I can see."

"So we can probably rule that out...maybe they're GPS coordinates?" Lilly asked.

"Don't start," Bernie countered.

"Okay, I have another serious thought. Maybe it's a navigational coordinate, they used the sextant back then."

"Oh, now there's good idea, I'll check it out," Bernie volunteered. He opened a website, said, "Wow, sextants are complicated. You need an index arm that aligns with divisions of the vernier and the arc. It looks like the verniers are the numbers. I'll load our Ansel numbers and see what comes up."

"That does sound complicated," Lilly replied. "Can you imagine having to rely on a sextant and you're in the middle of an Ocean? I wonder what happened when they encountered a bunch of cloudy days."

"No kidding, they could be way off course."

"Like us?"

"Probably. Here's what I found at north seventeen by west seventy-eight. We can buy an optic lens with seventeen times power, or a seventeen-point seven cubic foot refrigerator, or..." Bernie's playful demeanor shifted as he picked up his phone and zoomed in on the Ansel tombstone photo.

"What?" Lilly asked. "What are you thinking?"

"The decimal point made me wonder. I'm looking for a dot between the numbers in the picture. You know, like when it's used as a multiplication symbol. I don't see anything, but the stone is so weathered and covered with growth." He tapped on a calculator app and said, "The two numbers equal one thousand, three hundred, twenty-six."

They exchanged a knowing look.

Bernie almost shouted, "We just talked about that number as a date!"

"We did," Lilly replied. "I have it right here." She licked her thumb and quickly paged back through her notebook. "Here we go. That's the year Saint Peter moved the See from Vladimir to the Kremlin!"

They locked eyes, absorbed by the revelation.

Lilly tapped on her laptop, found a website, and read aloud, "Acknowledged in 1326, the seat of the Russian Orthodox Church moved from Vladimir, Russia, to the Kremlin in Moscow. The Church of the Assumption was the first stone cathedral built, along with palaces for the prince and leading boyars and monasteries."

"This is pointing to Moscow and specifically The Church of the Assumption," Bernie stammered.

"Looks like it, same name, different country. I think we're on to something solid, Bernie!"

They stopped talking to collect their thoughts, then Bernie shared a concern and asked, "When will this scavenger hunt end? I mean, what's after Moscow? Another city in another country? And, besides, can we even get into the Kremlin? Is it even open to the public since the Ukrainian War?"

"You might have to break in," Lilly interrupted, amused by Bernie's rant.

"What?"

"The Kremlin. You might have to break in," she teased. "After all, apparently we're spies, so they won't let us in."

"Ha, you think you're so funny."

"I do see your point, though," Lilly replied as her smile faded. "And how long do you think Attuchi will keep paying for our excursions?"

Bernie replied, "Not sure, but I don't think I'll contact him for a while. Let's think about this."

The following morning Bernie and Lilly unlocked the front door of the store just before nine and found Shandra and Katy standing behind the checkout counter chatting, ready for business.

"Good morning!" Shandra said loudly. "You don't need to relock it, everything's set-up.

"Oh, okay," Lilly replied, leaning over to turn on the neon open sign hanging in the window, then asked, "How's everyone today?"

Responses were favorable, and fresh brewed coffee awaited them in the break room.

Bernie and Lilly came out from the back, coffees in hand, and seeing no customers, joined in the discussion about knight's errantry at the counter.

Shandra said, "Katy and I were just talking about the chain mail armor you have coming."

"I can't wait to see it," Katy said with enthusiasm. "And the suit has provenance I hear?"

"It does. It's a cool piece," Lilly confirmed, then turned to Bernie, asked, "Where will you put it?"

Everyone looked around the store as Bernie replied, "Good question. Probably in one of the front displays so people walking by will see it." Everyone nodded.

"It should be a good draw to get people inside," Shandra said.

"Then price it so high it will never sell," Katy added. Everyone broke out laughing. Bernie replied, "That's a great idea, Katy. See? That's why I hired this woman."

Everyone admired Katy. She learned the ropes quickly and became adept at convincing customers they needed to walk out the door with an antique. On occasion, Bernie overheard Katy visit with potential customers using questions like, "And where do you picture this in your home?"
A brilliant tactic, yet so simple.

After the amusement with Katy calmed down, Lilly said, "Well I did some digging this morning on the Kremlin and specifically, their Church of the Assumption."

"Does that mean you two are going to Russia?" Shandra asked, breaking into a big smile. "And I get to run the store again?"

Bernie replied, "I don't think so, we..."

Lilly broke in, "That's just it, I'm pissed! There would be no reason to go. I found out the rebuilt cathedral from 1326 was allowed to be demolished by Communists in 1937."

Bernie added, "So, any further poems or clues were likely lost."

"Scattered to the wind," Katy added.

Their attention was drawn to the front of the store when three varying sized antique bells jingled in different pleasing tones. A well-dressed middle-aged woman walked in.

"Good morning!" Shandra said enthusiastically, then excused herself to wait on her. Katy followed as back up, increasing the odds for a sale.

Later that afternoon in the back room of the store, an eight-track tape played *It Was the Best of Times*, by Styx. An empty pizza box lay splayed open on the end of Lilly's worktable as she examined a wood-framed mantle clock, determining value but doubting her findings. The profit ratio appeared off.

"Hey Bernie, when you get a second, I have a question," she said.

Without looking up from examining a pair of gold earrings at his workstation, he replied, "Sure, just a minute." He entered a few numbers on his laptop and walked over to Lilly, asked, "What's up?"

"It's about the value of this Thomas clock," she said and pointed at his buying notes, then continued, "You bought an eighteen eighties Seth Thomas Adamantine, key wound, eight-day with bell strike in what appears to be working mint condition. I think we should list this for four seventy-five. My question, did you make a mistake listing what you paid for it?"

Bernie's face grew a broad smile as he replied, "No mistake. I bought this at an estate sale. I got there late. I couldn't believe it was still available. I offered seventy-five, we settled at a hundred. I anticipated a strong profit potential. Looks like I was right. I don't think they knew what they had."

"You are so lucky, you know that? You really are."

"Only because I have you, babe," Bernie said, then kissed her cheek.

She stood up and leaned into him, whispered, "I'm the lucky one."

They helped close the store at five, stopped by the bank with a deposit, then headed home.

After dinner, sitting on the couch, Lilly poked around different sites on her laptop, not paying much attention to the televised baseball game Bernie had on. Being stubborn and curious, she switched from Facebook to historical articles about the Kremlin, clicked on a site about Russian architecture and read, *The Assumption Cathedral was situated at Cathedral Square, surrounded by relics of other cathedrals and churches, examples of Old Russian architecture, including the Ivan the Great Belltower, the Facets Palace and the original Patriarch's Palace.*

The cathedral's loss leaves a historic void of epic proportions, having served for centuries as Russia's state and ritual center. Grand princes were proclaimed, Czars enthroned, and later emperors crowned there. *Inaugurations were held, government acts were read, and grand services were held.*

Seeing no clues, she clicked on the next site and read, *Archaeological digs from 1968 indicate the site of the former Church of Assumption was previously a medieval burial ground. Other evidence indicates a wooden church may have existed on the site in the 12th century. This was replaced by a limestone structure built in 1326. That structure was replaced in the 15th century and destroyed five hundred years later. Like this one, many buildings were damaged or destroyed by the communists' Bolshevik revolution of the early 20th century.*

Lilly sat back in thought, her pen getting a work-out on her lower lip. *I already know all that.*

"What'd you find?" Bernie asked without turning away from the game, knowing what the pen tap meant.
"Mostly stuff we already know. Who's winning?"

"Red Sox are up three to two in the bottom of the sixth. So, what do we already know?"

"I'm reading historical articles about the Kremlin about what has survived and changed over the years."

"Sounds familiar," Bernie replied, then returned his attention to the ball game.

Lilly, already on her third browser page with muddled subject lines, clicked on the next website, an obscure article from the Church Review magazine. She read, *In the Archangel Cathedral of the Moscow Kremlin, there are relics of forgotten church leaders, Saint Michael, Theodore of Chernigov, Prince Svetozar Vladimir, and Cardinal Dimitry Donskoyev.* Her breath caught, making her choke and cough.

Bernie sat up quickly and patted her back, asked, "You okay, babe?"

Lilly, tearing up a little, nodded slightly, and wheezed out a reply, "Excuse me!"

"Need me to do the Heimlich Maneuver, call nine-one-one, get you a glass of water?" Bernie asked, concerned, yet seeing she was still breathing, attempted some humor.

"No, I'm fine, but you have to check this out," she said with urgency, pointing at her screen as she got up to get some water. Lilly placed her laptop on the coffee table in front of Bernie, then headed to the kitchen.

"But the Braves just tied the score," Bernie said. "I'll read it in a minute. You're sure you're okay?"

"Yeah, my breath caught when I found the name, Vladimir, possibly from our Ansel tomb poem," Lilly said, trying to contain her excitement. She filled her glass and gulped it down.

"So not only a place, but a name linking to our poem?" Bernie asked skeptically, glancing down at her screen.

"Maybe," Lilly replied. "I found a guy buried in an article...a prince from Russia with the same name."

Bernie turned up the tv volume a notch. The analyst announced, "That's two down with Matao on second and here comes coach Houcher onto the field for a time out. Ok folks, we're going to take a quick break, but stay right where you are, we have a nailbiter!"

Bernie pushed the mute button. Lilly came back with two glasses of water and sat down, putting a glass in front of Bernie.

"Thanks, babe," he said, then leaned forward to read her screen.

After a minute, he sat up, asked, "What are the odds that this is our Vladimir?"

"I'll let you know when I know," Lilly replied.

The game resumed. Bernie turned the volume back on.

Lilly picked up her laptop, keyed in *Svetozar Vladimir,* then clicked on a promising looking article and read, *The name dates to 831 when Vladimir-Rusate ruled Bulgaria. Son of Donnar the Noble of Moscow. Reigned as the prince of Moscow from 1326 to 1359. Married to Daria who bore him three sons and three daughters.*

Lilly patiently watched the game with Bernie until the next commercial break, then she muted the tv, said, "Okay, I think I found the clue that has to be more than a coincidence."

Bernie leaned over, said, "Okay." He read the short article, sat back, and unmuted the tv for a toilet paper ad.

"What? You're just going to watch a commercial after reading those dates?" Lilly asked, sounding hurt.

Bernie turned up the volume and ignored her, not wanting to hear more of her logic.

Lilly pleaded her case, speaking loudly over the cartoon bears with cleaner tushes, asked, "Svetozar took over the year the Orthodox moved to Moscow in 1326. You don't think that's more than just a coincidence? He could be the link we need."

Bernie glanced at her, hit mute, asked, "Where would we look?"

Lilly replied, "There has to be records of his existence, Moridorno must have hidden something related to him in the Kremlin."

"Okay, I agree, but the Kremlin must be huge, where do we start?"

"Budapest is huge, and we found our way."

Bernie relented, said, "I'll contact Attuchi and see what he thinks. I'll also have him investigate possible restrictions we may have in Russia since things are still settling out after the war."

Lilly replied encouragingly, "I read an article this morning about how Russia has become more inviting to the outside world recently."

"Well, that's a plus."

Chapter 16

Moscow, Russia

Attuchi approved travel with the connections to Russia, so once again, Bernie planned for the store to run on cruise control for five days and booked flights. Worry lines furrowed his brow because he couldn't rid the image of the bloody bird from his head and couldn't bear to see blood on Lilly.

Three weeks later, a jet's wheels lifted off from the Huntington runway with Bernie and Lilly on board. Within an hour, the engines reduced power and they landed at LaGuardia airport for their connection to Moscow. At customs, the couple got questioned in depth about their incident in Germany but processed smoothly after that. They scanned in and walked on board. Because of their delay at customs, the cabin door closed right after they buckled into their first-class seats. As the plane achieved cruising altitude for the ten-hour flight, Bernie reclined his seat and tried to relax, but something bothered him. *How did the authorities at customs know so much about us?*

After two meal services and a few intermittent naps, Bernie and Lilly chatted about touring the Kremlin and its vast grounds and many buildings.

"I hope the Russians display at least some English," Bernie said.

"I'm sure they will have translations," Lilly assured him. "Or we can use our phones as usual."

Airplane cabin chimes sounded. A flight attendant announced preparations for descent. After a few minutes, rain streamed sideways on the windows as the plane lurched through a cloud layer, then intermittent lights appeared on the ground. The plane shuddered and decelerated rapidly, pitching her passengers forward, then veered off quickly and taxied at a snail's pace to gate D4.

Bernie and Lilly deplaned and followed the signs to customs with passports in hand. After a short wait, they stepped up to the counter where a young female attendant wearing gothic attire including black lipstick glanced from them to their passport pictures, then typed on her keyboard and read her screen.

Tilting her head slightly, she looked up at them with raised brows and said in a heavy Russian accent, "Wait here." She got up carrying their passports and went briefly into a back office, then stepped back out and waved, said, "Please, you will come."

Bernie and Lilly walked to the end of the counter and into the office. An older man in a suit sat behind his desk. He looked up when they entered.

"This is comandante Kalashnik," the attendant introduced them.

"Hello, please you will sit," the comandante said, motioning to the chairs in front of his desk, then looked at the attendant, said, "Thank you Ensign Poltov, you may return to your post."

The middle-aged comandante flashed a fake smile and with halting English, asked, "So, what brings you to Moscow?"

Bernie's thoughts clouded, asked, "Why are you detaining us? We already cleared customs before we boarded. We're just tourists who want to tour the Kremlin."

Comandante Kalashnik smiled condescendingly, cleared his throat, and replied, "It appears that is not always the situation with the two of you." He waved a hand across his open laptop and continued, "I see here you two have recently traveled frequently, making abrupt travel changes, you caused vandalism in Germany, and you have somehow made an enemy with the Catholic Church. You must admit, you appear highly suspicious. What are we to think Mr. Maynard and, is it miss Halpers?"

"Yes," Lilly replied timidly.

"For these many reasons you are now sitting in my office." He paused for effect, glancing back and forth at the young couple, then continued, "You are antique dealers?"

"Yes."

"Then why would you break into a private cemetery in Germany? Are not tomb stones too heavy to steal?" Kalashnik smiled at his humor.

Bernie remained stoic, and rattled off a reply, "Well, the fence was already broken, and we just let ourselves in. We were looking for a specific grave, and if you allow me to..."

"Mr. Maynard," Kalashnik interrupted. "We don't like westerners breaking in to remove our past treasures from our country." Then his voice raised, "Nor do we appreciate people digging around in our affairs. You two don't look like spies, but your behavior patterns certainly raise the possibility. So, perhaps your odd story is true, and you're not with the CIA. But I must say, if you are spies, you're not very good at your jobs because you reek of suspicion." Kalashnik paused for effect.

"We're not spies," Bernie said flatly.

Kalashnik continued, "I see here you are on a watch list by the Catholic Church. Tell me why."

Bernie and Lilly exchanged a questioning look. Bernie asked, "What kind of watch list? And what does religion have to do with customs?"

"The report I see here does not contain such details," the comandante replied, waving his hand across his computer screen again. "But whatever you are doing has drawn attention from our government, and somehow angered our friends at the Catholic Church."

Bernie and Lilly sat in silence.

"No comment, eh? My young visitors, I've been doing this a long time. So, now it's time for you to tell me the truth or I will not stamp your passports and arrange for immediate deportation. So, why are you really here?"

Bernie looked at Lilly for support but saw fear in her eyes. Even so, she gave him a small smile and a nod. Bernie said, "We were hired by an Italian law firm to look for clues imbedded in a letter written in fifteen eighty-two. We believe there may be related clues hidden somewhere in the Kremlin."

"I see," Kalashnik replied, drumming his fingers on his metal desk, then stopped and looked up, said, "The Kremlin is full of cathedrals, is that not more than a coincidence? And what specifically are you looking for?"

Bernie glanced at Lilly, said, "Go ahead, tell him."

Lilly replied, "We're specifically looking for information about a former Russian prince named, Svetozar Vladimir, who lived during the fourteenth century. We hope to find any records related to his reign."

Comandante Kalashnik sat back in his chair and looked a bit stunned, then intrigued, he said, "Young lady, at last, that sounds like truth. I pride myself in knowing the difference." After a few moments of indecision, Comandante Kalashnik continued, "Okay then, you two go do your research, but I'm putting in my notes you will not be allowed to extend your visit. I will have ensign Poltov stamp your pass books, but I caution you, we are not lenient like our German neighbors. If you break our laws, or are caught spying, you will suffer harsh consequences and you two won't be going home at all."

Free at last, Bernie and Lilly quickly found ground transportation to the Red Kremlin Hostel, near Red Square and within walking distance to the vast Kremlin grounds. Sitting in the back seat of their cab, Bernie leaned over and kissed Lilly on the check, then whispered, "I love you, Natasha. You're a brave woman."

She whispered back, "I love you too, Boris." With her hand resting on his leg, she slid her fingers up slowly. Bernie looked at her in surprise while she casually looked out the window and grinned.

Bernie leaned into her and whispered, "You are such a tease."

"I won't be later."

Sensing the electricity, the driver curiously glanced back at them through his rearview mirror. They drove through darkness along miles of deserted streets.

Finally reaching their hotel, the lobby looked deserted. Bernie glanced up at the digital clock behind the front desk: 3:40 a.m. *No wonder.*

After check-in, the couple found the accommodations compact, the bathroom shower stall quite narrow.

"Not exactly designed for two people to fit," Bernie commented.

"We can play Tetris," Lilly replied, with a wink. Bernie's left eyebrow shot up.

They settled in and gazed out their window at the colored flecks of light reflecting off the Moskva River.

Lilly suggested, "We should try to get some sleep."

"You're right. The clocks say it's almost four in the morning, but to us it's still seven the night before. We need to adjust."

They got ready for bed, climbed under the covers, and gave each other a kiss good night, then sleep became formally delayed.

The next morning, they were out the door by 8:45 in search of coffee and a bite. Just around the corner, they found the Korchma Cafe and sat at a table next to the front windows. A middle-aged waitress saw them come in. She smiled, said something in Russian and handed them menus.

"Hello," Bernie said, smiling up at her. "Do you by chance speak English?" She smiled and nodded, "Oh, ya, ya. Americans?" Turned out she knew about ten words, but fortunately, coffee and bagels were among them.

Bernie pushed his empty plate back and yawned, then opened his laptop and looked at a map of Moscow with roads radiating away from the Kremlin, creating what looked like a turtle shell.

"It's big," he said, pointing. "Looks like we are here. The State Library is literarily right across the street. See?"

"Yep."

"We can enter here, then walk to the Archangel Cathedral, since that's where relics of Vladimir might be. If we don't find anything there, we should check out the Manezh Exhibition Hall over here that has a variety of historic displays."

"Sure, those look like good places to start."

"Then, we can wander through Cathedrals up in through here."

"I had no idea Russians were so catholic," Lilly said. "Hey, look. There's the Place of Skulls. I wonder what that's about."

"We'll have to check it out," Bernie replied."

As they walked toward Red Square, Bernie looked up at the tall buildings and didn't notice the concrete flower planter.

"Son of a bitch," he cried out and bent over to assess the damage to his shin.

"Here let's sit down a minute," Lilly suggested and led him to a nearby bench. She pulled up his pant leg, exposing a one-inch gash just beginning to leak a little blood. Lilly dashed over to a nearby hotdog cart and quickly pulled out a handful of napkins, ran back, and compressed them on his wound.

"Think you'll live?" She asked.

"I think so. Thanks. I just need to watch where I'm going."

She slowly pealed back the napkins to inspect his wound and said, "It's not deep and looks more bruised than cut."

After a couple of minutes, the bleeding stopped. As they resumed walking, Lilly tossed a Euro into the vendor's tip jar.

"Thank you," she said with a warm smile.

The couple turned north, crossed a four-lane street, and within twenty minutes, neared their destination.

"There it is," Lilly said. "The sign says they open at ten."

"Well, it's now ten o'three," Bernie countered, pacing at the large base of cement steps. "So, they're late."

"Rejoice in hope, be patient in tribulation," Lilly replied.

"Psalms?"

"Romans." Lilly pointed to the sign above the door.

The lock clicked and the double doors swung open. A man dressed in a ground-length maroon robe with a white sash stepped out onto the landing at the top of the stairs and smiled at them, he said, "Obroye utro."

"Hello. Good morning," Bernie replied, and waved, not sure what the man said.

The clergyman's smile vanished, and he disappeared into the cathedral, pulling the doors closed behind him.

"Well, isn't he pleasant?" Lilly asked.

They walked up and entered the cathedral. Bernie said, "At least he didn't lock us out."

With no sign of the grumpy priest, they were alone, save for security cameras and the strange feeling of being watched. They looked around carefully for ten minutes as a few patrons entered and sat in pews, but the pair found no clues after making a few translations. So, with feelings of frustration and trepidation, they left and walked to the cavernous two story Mahezh Exhibition Hall packed with displays and artifacts stretching before them for what looked like a mile.

"We're screwed," Bernie mumbled, leaning on Lilly.

She leaned back into him and said with an amazed tone, "This place is as big as a sports stadium."

"I know, right? But we might as well get started."

Examining each statue, display and point of interest, four hours crept by.

Bernie mentioned, "Kudos to the Russians for adding an English version to most of their display presentations."

"No doubt, that shaved off a ton of time."

After a late lunch at an outdoor kiosk, they decided to tour the State Historical Museum's four floors of displays. Looking around at three floors of exhibits made the afternoon fade like the ink in an 1880 opera theatre program from the play, The Nihilists.

"It's almost five," Lilly said, sounding surprised, as they walked down the stairs toward the exit.

"We didn't get to the top floor," Bernie replied, looking at his map app while navigating the steps. "But we'll have a full day again tomorrow."

"So, what's next, finish up the fourth floor here, then tour more cathedrals?" Lilly asked, yawning, placing her hand over her mouth. "Oh, my jetlag is kicking in."

"I know, it's a brain strain reading so many displays. But sure, let's start back here tomorrow morning."

Willing herself to stay optimistic, Lilly prognosticated, "We'll find something."

On the walk back to their hostel, and having worked up a good appetite, they stopped at Stolovaya's Restaurant for a bowl of borscht, kotleti and buckwheat applesauce bread.

"That sure hit the spot," Bernie said as they left the restaurant.

"That bread tasted delish. Hey, do you hear that?" Lilly asked, tilting her head. Orchestral music danced lightly off the buildings. They followed the melody four blocks, finding a free concert at an open-air amphitheater and found a couple open spots to sit down on one of the long rows of wooden benches. Classics by Balakirev and Tchaikovsky filled the night air with riveting precision and crescendos. Two hours later, after stopping for ice cream, the weary couple returned to their room, ready for bed.

The next morning after a quick bite, they finished touring the fourth floor of the Historical Museum, then toured Saint Basil's and Epiphany Cathedrals. Seeing local patrons praying and counting beads made them feel at ease. Lilly noticed a man wearing a grey fedora with white bird feathers sticking up from the hat band flashing a glimpse of her youth, when her late grandfather wore a similar hat, and sometimes he let her wear it. Much too big, the hat fell past her eyes to her nose and smelled of sweat and tobacco.

Bernie noticed Lilly's distraction, asked, "Do you see something?"

"Just that man over there, his hat reminded me of my grandfather. He wore a hat like that."

They stopped for lunch at the Lauduree Café for sandwiches and iced tea, then wandered into the Alexander Garden and sat on a bench under broad shade trees.

"So, what's next?" Lilly asked. "A nap?"

Bernie didn't answer right away as he studied a map app. Lilly rotated a half turn on the bench to lay down, rested her head on Bernie's legs and closed her eyes.

"I'm reading about the Place of Skulls, we'll eventually get there."

After a brief rest, Lilly rotated off Bernie's lap as they got up and wandered slowly around Alexander's Garden. Not finding anything, they walked to Lenin's Tomb at Red Square, then toured the Place of Skulls.

"Legend says executions took place here, hence the name," Bernie said as they ambled around the large circular platform.

Lilly pulled on Bernie's arm, said, "Don't look know, but there's that man with my grandfather's hat over there. I just caught him looking at us."

"Which way?"

"To your left near the bike rack. It's the guy wearing the grey fedora."

Bernie surreptitiously rotated in a full circle and stole a glance at the man who had turned away, then suggested, "Maybe a coincidence? After all, there are a lot of tourists and locals around."

"I hope you're right."

Bernie checked his phone for the time, asked, "What do you think? It's four-thirty. We still have two places to check out, but I think I'm done for today. Besides, everything closes at five."

Lilly replied, "We didn't get as far as you wanted to, did we?"

"Nope."

"Sorry we haven't found anything." She reached down and held his hand as they walked, she asked, "What's left?"

"The Chamber of Saints and the Temple of the Righteous."

"That's not bad, at least we'll be able to finish your planned locations. We still might find something."

"True, but our odds are getting slim."

The following morning after breakfast at the Korchma Café, Bernie noticed a black van with tinted windows parked across the street. His senses awakened with a ripple of nervous energy but dismissed the thought as delusional paranoia from watching too many spy movies. *Like the Russians would apply high end resources like that for us.*

The pair walked to The Temple of the Righteous. Meandering through the three-story building consumed most of their morning, but they found nothing of significance in the multitude of exhibits.

Lilly checked the time and said with a shocked tone, "It's eleven thirty-two already."

"Time flies when you're having fun," Bernie replied, trying to sound optimistic.

"My feet hurt, Bernie. I should have packed two pair of tennis shoes."

"I know, mine are hurting too. But we're here, last day, and we can't give up," he said, and gave her a hug.

Lilly pulled back quickly to get a better look at a woman in a yellow dress staring at them from a distance. The women turned away when she met Lilly's eyes.

"What is it? What's wrong?" Bernie asked.
"Probably nothing...paranoia, I thought I caught that lady over there in the yellow dress staring at us. I'm just bushed, that's all."

"Well, I'll go talk to her and ask her."

Lilly grabbed his arm to stop him, asking with a stern voice, "Where are you going?"

He turned back slightly and replied, "I'm going to go say hello and prove she's just a local, or a tourist like us."

He turned back around, but the lady was gone. He walked briskly to where she had been seconds before and looked around. He looked back at Lilly, held up his arms and shrugged his shoulders.

"See? Nothing but your imagination, it's like she wasn't even there," Bernie said as he walked back with a mystified look. He added, "I know how you feel, I saw a black van this morning and immediately thought espionage with a team inside watching our every move."

"Maybe they are, Bernie."

Scrutinizing everyone around them, the pair walked to their last stop, The Chamber of Saints, a two-story building displaying history of the sixty-eight eparchies of the Russian Orthodox Church. The first floor yielded no pertinent clues, so they took the stairs to the second floor where each room held a themed exhibit. In the third room, behind several glass displays, they found framed correspondence and poetry written by past clergy. Some pages were yellowed with age, the ink faded.

Giving each other optimistic smiles, Bernie and Lilly got out their phones and loaded their translation apps and began to examine the various letters.

"How about I start this way, you head that way?" Bernie suggested.

"Sounds good."

Ten minutes passed when Lilly called out to Bernie. He found her hopping like a bunny in front of a display case. He walked over and peered in at the four framed pages propped up on small easels, then skimmed across the Russian words. The name, *Aditya,* jumped out from a poem second from the left. He felt a jolt of adrenaline. Lilly keyed in the words, then held up her phone with the full translation that read,

> *Cecilia's love for Aditya*
> *Could not absolve his sin*
> *She patiently guards*
> *His warm sun's rays*
> *　~anonymous in God's love*

On their way out, they stopped at a small gift shop to purchase souvenirs. The clerk spoke fair English, and thanked them for stopping in and did they have a good time?

"More than you'll ever know," Bernie replied in a jovial tone. The clerk turned her head slightly, wondering what he meant.

With the afternoon still young, Bernie and Lilly had time for more exploration or could even catch an antique store, but their feet would not comply. So, they headed back to their hotel, excited about their newfound poem. While waiting at a streetlight for the pedestrian blinking red hand to change into the white stick man, Lilly turned to Bernie and leaned into his chest. He wrapped his arms around her as she melted in, souvenir bags dangled from their hands.

"Damn, Bern, I'm so happy we found Aditya."

Bernie returned a halfhearted grunt as he became lost in thought, watching the pedestrian signal change from a solid red hand to a flashing red count-down, *twenty-five, twenty-four, twenty-three.*

Still thinking about her aching feet, Lilly asked reflectively, "Hey Bern?"

"Yeah?"

"Are you listening to me?"

"Yeah."

"Why did it have to be the last building before we found our next clue?"

"That's easy, Murphy's Law," Bernie replied, keeping an eye on the count down, *seventeen, sixteen.*

Lilly's mood changed, she asked thoughtfully, "Do you think we're being followed?"

"Sure feels like it sometimes, but Russia has always had that mystique for me."

Lilly asked, "What if we were real spies getting hunted by the KGB because we discovered a long-hidden secret about Aditya?"

"Can we have guns?" Bernie asked playfully. *Twelve, eleven, ten.*

"Hey, seriously. It sounds like fun...and I could write a book about our travels and the romanticism of the poems, about Moridorno's dark history.

Bernie gave her a small kiss on the cheek and replied dryly, "It would never get published."

"And why not?" Lilly asked, defensively, staring back at him.

Bernie's face grew a mischievous grin as he gently bumped his forehead into hers. Inches apart, they searched the depths of each other's eyes, he whispered, "Because it would be too sexy." He chuckled, then grabbed Lilly's butt, one cheek in each hand, then roughly pulled her hips into his.

Lilly gasped and looked around at their fellow bystanders who were trying not to look, she whispered, "Hey, mister, you're a naughty boy making a scene." She tucked a whisp of hair behind an ear.

Bernie smiled at his wonderful woman and moved his hands up into neutral territory, then glanced at the count down, *seven, six, five.*

Lilly whispered tenderly, "But I do love my naughty boy."

"I love you, too, my little book writer. By the way, what would the title be?"

"I'd call it...*Bernie's Collectibles*, of course."

"That's boring. You should call it something else."

Three, two, one, white stickman.

Back at the Hostel, Bernie waved his card over their door lock, the light flashed green and clicked open. They walked in to see their clothes strewn about the room, hanging from curtain rods like ghosts of de ja Vue. Bed covers lay wadded in a corner, their mattress pushed askew off the box springs. In the bathroom, toiletries were opened and scattered on the vanity. On the mirror, someone smeared toothpaste in large fingerpainted letters:

GO HOME

Several condoms were opened and partially filled with hand lotion. Tums were scattered on the floor, many stomped into powder. Someone defecated in the toilet but didn't flush. *Sick bastards*, Bernie thought. *It's getting worse.* He flushed the toilet. *Maybe I shouldn't have done that?*

After looking at the chaos, and holding back tears, Lilly visibly trembled and started to ramble, "Bernie, why are they doing this to us again? What do they think we have? What we are looking for? No, that's not it, because we don't know what we're looking for, so how can we have what they want?"

Bernie walked over to Lilly and embraced her tightly, feeling her nerves vibrating, he replied, "I don't have any answers, babe, but it's just stuff. They didn't hurt us or kill any birds this time."

Waiting in the lobby for the police, the shaken couple looked up every time the automatic sliding doors opened. To their relief, two male officers showed up within ten minutes. Returning to their room, the officers conducted a brief examination and took a lot of pictures. They had Bernie and Lilly arrange their belongings to determine if anything had been stolen. After a quick assessment, nothing appeared missing, so the officers filed a vandalism report and left. Bernie and Lilly repacked their suitcases and returned to the lobby. The hotel administration allowed a room change to one on the ground floor next to the lobby with complimentary toiletries.

Bernie and Lilly returned to their original room to retrieve their luggage. Bernie propped open the door with his suitcase while they took one more look around for stray socks. An older man in a black suit knocked on their open door.
"Knock-knock," he spoke in a heavy Russian accent, "May I have a moment of your time?" A grey-haired man with thin lips and a square chin stepped brazenly a couple paces into their room.

Surprised and a little scared, Bernie turned and yelled, "Hey, stop. Who are you?"

The man retreated one step back and leaned against the door frame.

"Pardon the intrusion," he replied sounding pleasant, then tipped his black hat and bowed slightly. "Please do not be alarmed, I am here as a friend." He paused and smiled; gold crowned several of his front teeth. His tone grew ominous. "I will take only a few moments of your time, and I'm afraid I must insist you listen."

Bernie and Lilly, standing on the far side of the room, gave each other a nervous glance.

"What do you want?" Bernie asked, trying to sound brave and defiant.

"Are you with the police?" Lilly asked hopefully.

"My name is Victor Blevensky. I am from the Kremlin and have knowledge you two were warned by Comandante Kalashnik at customs about snooping, yet you persist for the past three days going here and there about the Kremlin. What are we to think?"

"We're just tourists," Bernie replied, speaking slowly for effect, trying to sound calm.

"You keep saying that. Can't you come up with something more imaginative? You two are poorly trained."

"When will you people stop being so suspicious?" Bernie asked. "We are not spies."

Blevensky took off his hat and looked down at his feet, then tapped his heels together like Dorothy in the Wizard of Oz. He looked up, asked, "What did you find today in the Chamber of Saints?"

Bernie and Lilly froze. The hair on the back of Bernie's neck stood up as he stammered, "Well, we...we found some poems and historic letters."

A noise drew their attention to the hall. A housekeeper pushed a supplies cart by the propped open doorway as the three looked out and watched her. Bernie contemplated calling out, but Blevensky held a finger to his lips and shook his head slightly as the housekeeper passed. Blevensky continued, "So, as I was saying, we visited with our German neighbors and our catholic friends." He looked down at his shoes and tapped his heels again, then looked up with his eyes screwed back tightly, he said, "Whatever you are looking for, there is no vat of gold as you may think. You were warned, and now, you see? Trouble follows you when you stray too far from home."

"So, are you the one who trashed our room?" Bernie inquired sternly, masking his fear.

Blevensky chuckled and picked small bits of lint from his suit jacket, he replied, "No, I don't like to get dirty. But I do know it's a dangerous city, and we find it difficult to control such petty crimes. Good thing you were gone, so no one got...hurt. Perhaps you should consider returning to your home country."

"We fly out tomorrow," Bernie replied flatly. "But I suppose you already know that."

"Be sure you catch your flight," Blevensky replied, turned on a heel and left the room. Bernie quickly moved his suitcase and locked the door.

"I want to go home now," Lilly said, letting go full sobs into Bernie's chest, making two wet spots on his shirt.

"Tomorrow, babe, tomorrow," Bernie assured.

Even with their reassigned room near the lobby, Bernie slept with a hair dryer that night, the closest thing he found that might serve as a weapon. The pair found a meager solstice during a long night when every small noise stirred them from tepid sleep. Four a.m. crawled into place when they sprung out of bed like firemen responding to an alarm.

At the airport, Bernie and Lilly found a sliver of irony as they breezed through customs, found their gate, and waited an hour for boarding, glancing suspiciously at every fellow traveler. Once in the air, sitting pampered in first class, their fears subsided on imaginary padded clouds as sleep and dreams captivated many hours of their long flight home.

Chapter 17

Rome, Italy

The fireplace bricks felt warm long after the fire left black, smoldering embers. Cardinal Beufort stood up, rotated his laptop for everyone to see, then started the surveillance footage of Bernie and Lilly at the Kremlin in the Chamber of Saints. His canonist and Attorney Tubero were seated at a small conference table and watched Lilly stop in front of a glass case and begin to hop.

Cardinal Beufort said, "You can see how excited they become at that specific display case, so our regents examined the four poems inside. One poem used the name, Aditya."

"A name in the Moridorno letter, as I recall," Attorney Tubero said.

"Exactly. Here is the poem we believe caused their excitement," Cardinal Beufort said, as he slid a printed page across the table to Tubero. "They are definitely on the right track."

Tubero shared the page with the canonist, and they read,

Cecilia's love for Aditya
Could not absolve his sin
She patiently guards
His warm sun's rays
        ~anonymous in God's love

Tubero asked, "So, what are we to make of this?"

"Mainly, we know they continue to successfully discover clues. With this last one, well, in effect, this proves the Moridorno letter does in fact contain information."

"Who's Cecilia?" Tubero asked.

The canonist spoke up, "Cecilia is a girl's name of Latin origin meaning blind, and the name of several cathedrals named after Saint Cecilia, our patron saint of music."

"Okay, good, good. It could allude to something to do with music and perhaps a blind love for Aditya," Cardinal Beufort speculated.

"We're still working on what it all could mean, my lordship."

Tubero asked, "What should we do with Maynard and Halpers?"

"I've been told to change our strategy," Beufort replied.

"What? Why?" Tubero asked. "I heard our Russian ally had them petrified."

"Primarily, we must continue to distance ourselves from any link to the missing hiker. Alfonse's widow continues to keep his case active, stirring up trouble, asking questions. And the tabloids persist with articles linking him to Moridorno and Satanic worship."

"So, what's our next move?" Tubero asked.

"Our tactics will change from deterrence to surveillance only, so no more direct contact. Our higher office is as curious as I am about what they might find next. We'll let out some leash, but make sure our field regents use strict diligence to stay out of sight."

"I'll make sure of it," Tubero replied.

"Let's move on," Cardinal Beufort said as he turned to his canonist, asked, "What's the next case?"

"Putnam and Horn, my grace."

Chapter 18

Huntington, West Virginia

For Bernie and Lilly, the routine of work and daily life felt therapeutic. Out of caution and lingering paranoia, Bernie decided to tell his parents about their room getting trashed, causing a burst of questions and concern.

"Just keep an eye out for anything suspicious," Bernie cautioned, the best advice he could give.

His dad countered, "When you shake a bee's nest, you're bound to get stung."

At the store, sales had been modest. Although there were a few bare spots on the store's shelves. Bernie gave Shandra and Seth a well-deserved paid two-week vacation, scheduling his dad, Katy, and Lilly, as needed to work the sales floor, plus keep up with online sales. A week after their return from Russia, Bryson and Chris invited Bernie and Lilly over for a poolside barbeque to hear about their recent adventure.

The following Sunday evening, after a fine meal, the plates were pushed back and empty except for crumbs and waded napkins. Bryson, Chris, and Grandma Fran sat spellbound while Bernie and Lilly shared stories and photos from their recent trip.

Bernie told the part where the ominous gold-toothed man invited himself into their room. "Then he alluded that we were looking for something that doesn't exist. What did he say, Lilly?"

"There is no vat of gold. We would say pot of gold."

Fran asked, "But you're not looking for gold, are you?"

Bernie chuckled and shook his head, said, "Grandma, we still have no idea what we're looking for." He looked at Lilly and asked her, "Should we tell them?"

Lilly looked around the table, then at Bernie and replied demurely, "It's up to you."

"Well, now you have to tell us," Bryson demanded, sitting forward in his chair.

Chris looked up quickly and caught Lilly's eye with a surprised, but happy, questioning expression. Fran looked on, too, with a knowing look. A modest smile crossed Lilly's lips as she looked back at Chris, then glanced modestly at Fran. Lilly shook her head slightly. *No, not a pregnancy.*

The men didn't even notice the silent question and answer that passed among the women. Lilly noticed the brightness fade slightly from Chris's eyes. Fran looked relieved.

Bernie explained, "We determined the probable meaning of the poem we found at the Kremlin leads us next to Albi, France."

"What? So quickly?" Bryson asked.

Chris leaned forward and leaned her elbows on the patio table, asked, "So, are you going there next?"

Bernie and Lilly looked at each other with knowing smiles, then Bernie replied, "Probably, but not for a while. At least a month."

"The gold-toothed man convinced us to take a break," Lilly said. "He creeped me out."

"And we're kind of burnt out from being on the go so much," Bernie added.

"Oh, boo-hoo, you poor world travelers," Bryson teased, and laughter ensued.

"So, what did you sleuths find out that's leading you to France?" Fran asked.

Bernie replied, "I'll let Lilly explain."

"We found the name, Aditya, in a poem at the Kremlin," Lilly began. "Which is a name that directly links to the Moridorno letter. Seeing that name tipped us off to a specific poem we found in the Chamber of Saints. Next, I Googled other key components in the lines, starting with Cecilia, really the only other line in the poem with a good reference point. Anyhow, I found her name in a religious sense originated from Saint Cecilia, the patron saint of music. So, I looked up Saint Cecilia and found she's named for several cathedrals around the world. During our search in Budapest, we found a reference in a census book that showed Hugot Ansel, another name in our search, went on sabbatical somewhere in France."

"So, that's two references that point to France," Bernie added. "Now, there are two Saint Cecilia Cathedrals in France. One in Trastevere, the other's in Albi, but my friend, Sean, mentioned Father Fionscetti served in Albi, so we're starting there. If we strike out, we're preapproved by Attuchi to make a stop in Trastevere."

"What's Albi near?" Fran asked.

"It's southern France, just north of the Spanish border, along the Tarn River," Bernie replied.

"Aren't you concerned about the threats?" Chris asked. "I'm getting worried about you kids. Are you getting in over your heads?"

Bryson jumped in, said, "That's a good point, sounds risky, and say you go to Albi and Trastevere and find another poem with a clue with another name or whatever, and that leads you to another country, then another. When does it stop?"

Bernie and Lilly gave each other a worried look, then Bernie replied, "I guess when we stop finding clues." He glanced around the table, then added, "Or Attuchi's client cuts off funding!"

Bryson replied, "Kids, you might be travelling a long time with that fat bank account!" He caught Lilly's eye and gave her a wink.

"You two be careful," Fran said as she dabbed a handkerchief on her forehead. "I wish you would slow down and reconsider. I worry every minute when you travel overseas lately."

"Don't worry Gramma Fran," Lilly said. "Bernie has our backs." Bernie's left eyebrow shot up.

Chapter 19

Albi, France

Six weeks later, Bernie and Lilly landed smoothly at the Albi-Le Sequestre airport, but then things got bumpy. With luggage in tow, they were led into a cramped customs office to answer Inspector's Bescond's questions.

"We're here for a total of four days, counting today," Bernie replied politely. "We fly out on the ninth."

"And for what reasons do you pay us a visit?"

"We're planning to tour Saint Cecelia's Cathedral tomorrow, the next day we drive to the Mediterranean coast."

Lilly's head snapped up and curiosity etched her face as she stared at Bernie. The inspector picked up on her body language, and asked with a heavy French accent, "Miss Halpers, this perhaps is news for you, yes?"

Lilly smiled nervously and stammered, "I...I hadn't been told about the drive to the coast." She looked at Bernie for answers.

Bernie replied, "It was a surprise." He turned to Lilly and gave her a small smile, said, "Surprise." Looking back at the inspector, he continued, "We'll be back in Albi on the third day, then we fly out the morning after that."

"Where on the coast are you going?"

"Agde."

The corners of Lilly's mouth rose slightly.

"And where are you staying here in Albi?"

"At the..." Bernie paused, trying to remember, then asked, "May I look at my phone?" The inspector nodded.

Bernie found the site, said, "We're at the Dormir Petit de Jeuner. I probably didn't say that right."

"Ah, le Dormir Petit de Jeuner," the inspector repeated crisply. "A very quaint bed and breakfast. I'm sure you will enjoy the hospitality. I've heard good things."

Lilly shot another surprised glance at Bernie.

Noticing Lilly's inuendo again, the inspector asked, "Ah, I see, perhaps another surprise? How do you say, I've let the cat out of the sack, no?"

"Bag," Bernie corrected.

"What?"

"Let the cat out of the bag, not sack. Never mind. I have no more surprises."

The inspector's smile faded. He tossed their dossiers on his desk and sat up, said, "Look, you two cause trouble in Germany, then Russia, what are we to think?"

"We didn't do anything wrong in Russia," Bernie countered.

"They trashed our hotel room," Lilly added.

"Yes, that sounds unfortunate, but frankly, you stink of suspicion. There's something more you do not say to me. I can tell, I'm very good at my job. So, you now have a red flag in our system, and we will keep an eye on you."

"Fine, go ahead and follow us or whatever, we're getting used to it," Bernie challenged. "Is there anything else, or can we go now?"

The inspector paused and shot them each a firm look, said, "Yes, you are free to go, but you will not cause trouble in our country, right?"

The couple nodded as Inspector Bescond aggressively stamped their passports and slid them to the front of his desk.

Retrieving their credentials and luggage, the couple left the office in haste, and headed for transportation. As they walked through the terminal, Lilly leaned over and gave Bernie a peck on the cheek without losing stride.

"What was that for?"

"For the surprises. The coast sounds wonderful."

"It should be fun!" Bernie replied with a warm glow.

At the rental agency, Bernie signed the rental paperwork for the Fiat, found their car, then followed the blue arrow on the map app.

"How far is Agde from Aldi?" Lilly asked.

"Not far. I can't remember kilometers, but it's about a two-and-a-half-hour drive."

"That's not bad. We can explore along the way. What's day three look like for us?"

"Well, we'll have a leisurely morning on the coast, then drive back, so not much really. I have us back in Albi at le Dormir Petit de Jeuner for our last night.

"Sounds like fun, Bern."

They soon pulled into the driveway at the bed and breakfast. Bernie repeated the name in an exaggerated French accent attempting to mimic inspector Bescond. He followed the signs to park in the back and pulled into an empty stall. Rear house lights came on as a woman in her fifties stepped out on the back porch.

"Hello!" She spoke good English. "You must be the Americans?"

"That's right," Bernie replied.

"You're the last to arrive. Welcome, my name is Annette," she said with her slight accent, and seemed genuinely pleased to see them. "Come on in and make yourselves at home."

"Thank you," Lilly said smiling at Annette, who led them up narrow stairs to their room.

"Here we are," she said. "After you get settled in, downstairs the reading room is open until ten, and there's a small kitchenette for tea. I'll see you in the morning for breakfast at eight thirty. If you need anything else, call this number." Annette handed them a laminated page with instructions and bid them a good night.

A Queen Anne bed took up most of the room, with cramped space remaining for a dresser and rocking chair. The bathroom looked updated with modern fixtures.

"They must have punched into an adjacent room to create this much space," Bernie speculated as he looked around the bathroom.

"You're right, and I'll bet there wasn't indoor plumbing when this house was built."

Bernie opened a small door on the back wall expecting to see a closet with towels and spare toilet paper, but instead discovered a sauna. Lilly peeked in, "Another surprise, Bern?"

"Yes, for both of us. I didn't see this on their web site."

"Nice bonus," Lilly commented, then asked, hanging her arms over his shoulders, "Should we see if this thing works now, or later?"

"Hmm...I'm not sure," he replied, leaning in to kiss her on the mouth. She put her hands around his head and pulled him in tighter. Bernie pulled back, asked, "I'm thinking now?"

"Now is good."

"Okay, I'll fire this up and get it nice and hot...like you."

Ten minutes later they sat naked on towels and started to sweat. The thermometer read 135 Fahrenheit. Bernie got up and poured water on the rocks making them hiss and billow steam, shooting the mercury to 143. Returning to sit down, Bernie gazed at Lilly's slender legs, then up to her small nest of hair, her little pouch stomach, her pert breasts, and such a pretty face, then he noticed she was staring at his growing erection. Bernie still felt easily aroused by her sensual body. All it took was to see her naked.

He sat down next to her and asked, "This is cozy, huh? Or, too hot?"

"I'm getting used to it," she replied. "I haven't been in a sauna since college."

He leaned in and kissed her lightly and felt the smoothness of her mouth, then reached up for her. She reached down for him. Their sweat made their skin slippery. She stood up, ducked her head for the low ceiling and turned around, extending her arms against the wall for support. He glided smoothly in as she pushed back, and their breathing became rhythmic and labored. The heat enveloped them, and Lilly cried out, softly and slowly at first.

The next morning, the inn provided an impressive breakfast with eggs, ham, crepes, croissants, and a variety of jams.

"I think I ate six crepes," Bernie said, patting his stomach during their drive to Saint Cecilia's cathedral. Following his map commands, and after checking the rear-view mirror often, he turned into the large parking lot. A solid brick structure stood before them, appearing more like a castle than a church.

"Looks ominous, doesn't it?" Bernie asked.

"She looks solid, that's for sure," Lilly replied.

A blue sedan pulled in behind them and parked toward the back of the lot. Its driver slouched low and watched Bernie and Lilly walk into the cathedral.

Bernie and Lilly decided to first explore the perimeter grounds, then stopped at a kiosk and read,

Designed as an impregnable brick fortress, Saint Cecilia's cathedral is a symbol of catholic power against heretics and infidels. Built during a time of religious strife, the exterior has few ornate features, making the structure the most distinctive medieval cathedral in Europe. The interior is ornate with intricate tile and stonework typical of revolutionary gothic architecture.

The pair entered the cavernous interior, looking up simultaneously with mouths agape at the ceilings that rose into pinnacles. Colorful tile adorned the walls with heavenly scenes of white, billowy clouds on a blue sky above the browns and greens of a terracotta earth. A few people sat in the vast array of pews. *Probably locals*, Bernie thought. Two clergy talked quietly near the front pulpit, then disappeared through a side door. Bernie and Lilly wandered around reading and translating inscriptions on the walls for a half hour but found no discernable clues. Observing two different alcoves roped off to the public, Bernie decided to ask if a tour might be possible. He walked to the pulpit area to ask a young clergyman.

"Excuse me," Bernie said quietly. "Do you speak English?"

The young man, dressed in white with a ruffled collar, turned and replied in a heavy accent, "Yes, how may I help?"

"Do you offer tours?"

"I have seen it, but I am only a novitiate. I will go ask for you."

"That would be very helpful, thank you," Bernie replied.

The young man disappeared through a side door and shortly returned with a tall thin man in his mid-forties, wearing a white robe and a black biretta with a center pom. Thin round wire-rim glasses hung low off his narrow, beaked nose.

The novitiate gave a brief introduction to the father and walked away.

"Hello and welcome," Father Pierre Lavasseur said warmly.

They shook hands as Bernie introduced himself and Lilly.

Father Lavasseur spoke next, "So, I understand you wish for a tour?"

"Yes, would that be possible?" Bernie asked.

"We do at times give tours depending on circumstances, of course."

"We would greatly appreciate your time," Lilly replied.

"Of course, but I'm curious, what brings you to Saint Cecilia?"

Bernie replied in a friendly tone, "We're history buffs, antique dealers by trade." Bernie looked up and waved his hands in the air, added, "This place is so impressive."

"It is indeed," Father Lavasseur replied. "So, you are not seeking anything specific? Like perhaps a deeper relationship with Christ?"

"Well, not exactly," Bernie replied sheepishly. "We're mostly interested in wall inscriptions and poetry, that sort of thing."

Father Lavasseur replied, "There is some of that, but not too much that is inscribed on walls. I can show you around right now if you..."

Catching their attention, the side door moaned open as old hinges cried out for oil. They turned to see an elderly man with a stooped back walk slowly over to them thumping his cane on the floor with each step. Ignoring Bernie and Lilly, the ancient clergyman addressed Father Lavasseur and spoke French in hushed tones. Then with an unfriendly glance toward the visitors, he turned and thumped his way back through the side door like he wanted to wake the devil.

Father Lavasseur looked displeased, and said, "I'm terribly sorry, but I will not be able to give you a tour after all. Monsignor Dubaux needs some immediate assistance."

"We can come back later," Bernie postured.

"I'm sorry," Father Lavasseur replied. "I'm afraid no tours will be available."

Bernie and Lilly glanced at each other, not sure of what happened.

"But...why not?" Bernie asked.

"I'm sorry, Monsignor Dubaux does not approve."

"Is there any way I can change his mind? Perhaps a donation."

Father Lavasseur smiled, said, "I'm quite sure there is not. He was very clear with his directions. And I'd rather that you gave with an open heart rather than a bribe."

Bernie and Lilly exchanged a defeated look. Lilly whispered something to Bernie.

"What?" he whispered.

"Tell him about the letter," Lilly encouraged.

Bernie looked at her, contemplated, then nodded and turned to Father Lavasseur.

"We'd like to share something with you before we leave."

"Of course," Father Lavasseur replied, motioning to an empty pew. "What's on your mind?"

In hushed tones, Bernie laid out the story, starting with their employment with the Attuchi firm, the Moridorno letter and the subsequent poems leading to their travels. Bernie glanced at Lilly for support as he spoke. She nodded on que and glanced into the priest's kind eyes.

Bernie concluded, "And so, we have been led here. I realize this all sounds...farfetched."

Father Lavasseur sat back with his hands folded in his lap, then stared up at the lofted ceiling as if seeking divine answers. After a few moments, he rotated his body toward them and looked directly at the young couple, said, "There is something that rings true with some of what you say." He paused and shifted his weight again, then continued, "After all, this cathedral was built for the persecution of heretics and blasphemers, so these walls share with God many sad stories throughout the centuries."

Bernie and Lilly leaned forward. "And?" Bernie coaxed, "What rang true?"

Father Lavasseur replied, "That some physical evidence of sin was kept here at Saint Cecilia during medieval times."

"Evidence? Do you know what it might be?" Lilly asked, trying to contain her excitement.

"No, there were no specifics. I heard the story shortly after I arrived at Cecelia. But it was looked upon as more of a myth than a reality."

"Could this evidence still be here, perhaps hidden or locked up?" Bernie postulated.

"No, I have seen nothing, and to my knowledge, nothing unusual has ever been found. The church has had renovations and repairs over the years...some long before the seventeen years I've served here. Life gives us future stories to create while we follow stories from the past. Perhaps the story you follow contains a metaphorical lesson. Sin has been locked away within our Cecelia's walls to provide the love and comfort we all crave. Many stories in the bible test our strength and convictions, so I do find your journey pleasing that the lord through my ancient predecessor led you here, and may you go in peace to find what you seek."

Bernie and Lilly leaned forward in the pew with slumped shoulders and stared at each other, worried their search in Albi had been squashed so quickly, while absorbing the mini sermon they just received. Father Lavasseur looked at the young couple and felt a pang of guilt for not allowing them to see for themselves, to leave with a clear mind. He felt impelled to help, and said in hushed tones, "Listen, Monsignor Dubaux will soon be out of town for a few days. Can you come back on Saturday? Although I have great respect for him, I sometimes seek answers from a higher power. I will provide a quick tour so you may see for yourselves there is nothing here to find."

Bernie and Lilly looked up and nodded enthusiastically.

"Yes, Saturday is perfect," Bernie said. "Thank you so much. Would eleven be okay?"

"Yes, that's fine, any time before three."

Chapter 20

Agde, France

"The Agde exit is coming up next," Lilly warned, as Bernie merged the Fiat into the right exit lane, then got off the D612 and onto Cours des Gentilhommes to Le Belle Road, which lead them to their beach side resort.

After checking in, they walked along the sandy path to cabin six, with the Mediterranean's waves gently lapping the beach only yards away from their front door.

"This is awesome," Lilly said, pointing at the shards of sunlight sparkling off the crystallin sand. "Let's go for a walk and check out the shops down there."

"Sure, that sounds like fun," Bernie replied, then turned around and peered out at the blue-green sea.

Inside the cabin, turtle patterns adorned the curtains, a boat's wheel hung on the back wall above a queen-sized bed. A sign on the back wall read, *Life's a Beach*.

"It's perfect, Bernie," Lilly said, giving him a hug.

They unpacked a few things, put on sunscreen and flip flops, then strolled along the beach, letting the waves wash over their lower legs. Bernie picked up a few seashells, shared their intrigue with Lilly, then tossed them back onto the wet sand. After passing by a few hotels and resorts, they entered a stretch of beachside restaurants and retail shops. Bernie stopped at a small kiosk that offered parasailing.

"I've never done this, but it looks like fun. What do you think?" Bernie asked Lilly.

The young man in the kiosk handed them a brochure and explained the mechanics of windsurfing behind a boat. Bernie read his name tag, *Gregor.*

"Oh my gosh!" Lilly said excitedly. "Sure, this has always looked like fun."

Bernie bought tickets for the two o'clock launch at Pier Ten.

"It's about 50 meters down the beach, can't miss it," Gregor said, pointing.

Bernie asked him for lunch suggestions and the pair were soon seated under an umbrella at the Salty Tuna. The sea breeze felt good against their browning skin.

After Mai-Tais and crab nachos, they browsed through a few shops. Lilly bought an Agde t-shirt, Bernie, a hat. They showed up at Pier Ten, five minutes early, found their boat, and introduced themselves to the three-person crew. Shortly after heading out on open water, Bernie's new hat blew off, but luckily it stayed in the boat. He folded the hat lengthwise and crammed it between the seats.

Out in open water, the shoreline appeared thin on the horizon when the twin engines were reduced to idle. Bernie burped and re-tasted a vile combination of his lunch and Mai-Tais. He eyed the side of the boat, ready to heave-ho if necessary.

The crew conversed in French and pointed in different directions until their intonation shifted to mutual conclusion. The captain engaged the engines and turned the twenty-eight-footer into the wind while Bernie and Lilly got strapped into their harnesses. Bernie watched closely and listened for the distinctive clicks as the heavy metal latches engaged. He looked down at the bolts connecting the reel frame to the floor, then up to the large roll of thick white rope in front of them that would soon have them tethered two hundred feet above the water. Everything looked secure, but what did he know? He couldn't shake his nerves and felt like a kid waiting in line for the Zipper at the carnival. He glanced at Lilly and gave her a weak smile. She smiled back like she didn't have a care in the world, joking with Raul and the other crew. *How does she do that*? he wondered. The crew gave each other a thumbs up.

"Okay you two love birds," Raul told them with a heavy accent and began pointing to harness ropes, "Remember to hold here, and here to stay balanced, yes?" Bernie and Lilly nodded and positioned their hands.

"If you detect a problem or feel too nervous or unwell, pull out this red flag from the pouch here. I will see it, and bring you in, yes?"

They nodded.

Raul looked at the pair as he gave each harness a final tug. Having done this many times, Raul sensed Lilly's confidence and Bernie's unease, so he added, "Rest assured, we have done this many times without losing a single person." He gave them a big smile. "So, you two relax, have some fun. You can see for miles the pretty horizons."

Raul grabbed a rail, turned toward the front of the boat, and gave a thumbs up. The engines let loose a small roar as the boat picked up speed. Bernie and Lilly lurched back as the parasail popped fully open behind them. Raul put his hand on the release lever and pushed it down. The pair gently lifted off and Bernie's fears disappeared into the panorama.

They shared twenty minutes of exhilaration before the rope slowly reeled them back to reality and the confines of gravity. The bumpy ride back to the pier was no problem for Bernie's stomach with his adrenalin pumping and mind racing. He tipped the crew well as they disembarked. One of the crew chased Bernie down the pier to return his hat he forgot tucked between the seats.

Recommended by the boat crew, Bernie and Lilly dined at Les Tresors du Restaurant de la Mer that night. Bernie ordered the sea bass, Lilly, seared scallops, and they shared bites, tipping back their heads with each butter-dipped morsel.

After dinner, they meandered back to their cabin and donned swimsuits, Lilly wore a bikini. Wading into the sandy bottomed sea, they found a secluded place up the beach from the cabins. Standing chest deep, with arms draped over each other's shoulders, Lilly pointed to the inland hillside as the sun cast various orange colors of sunset. Bernie pointed in the other direction, to the sea's horizon, at the setting sun just peeking over dark clouds interrupted by whisps of striated lightning.

Bernie whispered in playful, conspiratorial tones, "Natasha, do you suppose we're being watched?" They scanned the sand and watched a couple walking in the distance, they heard faint music and laughter waft over the sea air from the beachside bars. The nearby cabins stood still and quiet.

Lilly replied with a mock accent, "Well, Boris, it appears we are quite alone, but if a French agent is hiding in the shadows, perhaps we should make it worth his trouble."

"I like the way you think, Natasha."

That said, their suits were soon held perilously in one hand leaving a free hand to explore. Lilly wrapped her legs around Bernie's torso. A large wave hit their shoulders and splashed up over their heads, knocking them off balance. Bernie wiped the water from his face and checked the shoreline. *Good*, he thought, *still no one around*. Lilly resumed her leg wrap as they rocked gently to the rhythm of the ocean.

Chapter 21

Albi, France

Bernie rose early to a windless new day and gazed at the flamingo pink sky reflecting off the glassy sea. Lilly joined him for a short walk along the beach. After coffee and bagels, they packed, and said good-bye to their coastal oasis. Bernie exited into Albi shortly before ten-thirty and drove straight to the cathedral.

Parking quickly and entering, the pair walked briskly toward the middle of the church and found a young clergyman; Bernie explained their appointment. The novitiate walked across the altar, and out the side door. Bernie and Lilly walked to the front and fidgeted. Bernie began to pace, then asked, "Do you think he forgot?" Lilly shrugged and puckered her mouth.

Finally, the squeaky side door opened, and Father Lavasseur emerged with a serious look on his face. But upon seeing the young couple, he smiled as he approached and shook their hands earnestly, said, "Good day, my friends. Good to see the Lord has brought you safely back. I apologize for the delay. I had some business..."

"No problem," Bernie replied, relieved the father materialized. "It's nice to see you again."

"Did you enjoy your stay in Agde?" Father Lavasseur asked.

"We had a really good time," Lilly replied. "A beautiful area, just as you said."

"Wonderful," Father Lavasseur replied, then clapped his hands and rubbed them together vigorously. "So, shall we begin your tour?"

"We are looking forward to it," Bernie replied.

"Okay, right this way, s'il vous plait," Father Lavasseur said as he held out an arm. "We'll start with the side corridors, then tour the administrative areas. We'll make a large circle through the back rooms."

He led them past two meeting rooms, a private chapel, sleeping areas, a large kitchen, and bathrooms. During the tour, the sleuths asked Father Lavasseur to translate a couple wall inscriptions, but nothing stood out that matched names or references. As they entered a modern looking area, Father Lavasseur explained, "This is part of a recent renovation, so everything here is quite new."

They walked through meditation rooms, a complex of large plush offices, more bathrooms, and a lounge with a kitchenette. They returned to the sanctuary through the squeaky side door.

"Here we are, back in the sanctuary," Father Lavasseur said with a touch of finality.

He noticed the looks of disappointment and offered solace, "I'm sorry...I deeply feel your sadness. We all search for reasons beyond our mortal existence. But like I said, there is not much out of the ordinary in our humble cathedral unless you seek God's reassurances. In that I can help."

A reverent silence followed, then Bernie asked, "You're sure there is nowhere else to look? Maybe artifacts were stored in the attic?"

"I'm afraid not," Father Lavasseur replied. "Everything's been updated for building codes. The Notre Dame fire caused us to examine our vulnerabilities."

Bernie put his hand on his chin and rubbed it like a genie lamp, then asked, sounding desperate again, "Are there any outbuildings or sheds on the property?"

Father Lavasseur smiled forgivingly and replied, "There is but this one glorious cathedral..." his voice trailed off and his expression changed. "I...I hadn't thought of this earlier, but there is a place we haven't yet seen. There's a small vacant room not accessible from inside. I've been down there only once years ago."

"May we see it?" Lilly asked, trying to contain her excitement.

"I don't see why not," Father Lavasseur replied. "I was told the room originally stored wood, then coal, then it was last used as a repair room. I must warn you, it's been abandoned for years, so there may be rodents and spiders."

"We'll take our chances, right, Lilly?"

She nodded, said, "If we find spiders, I'll bring them outside and set them free."

Father Lavasseur laughed, said, "I'm afraid that's about all you will find. As I recall, the room is quite empty."

"That's okay, we'd still like to take a look," Bernie replied. "Never hurts to keep trying."

"We can only hope," Lilly added. "We've come all this way."

"Hope is a great comfort," Father Lavasseur replied. "It gives each day a reason to be lived." He led them down a corridor and through a side door to the sidewalk outside. Turning right, they walked along the soaring brick wall and stopped near the southwest corner at a sturdy wooden door with wide metal banding bolted to its girth. A pull handle was fastened between two deadbolt locks spaced about eight inches apart. Father Lavasseur began testing his keys, one at a time. After a few failed attempts, a key not only made the wonderful sound of sliding into place but rotated. The same key opened the second deadbolt and Father Lavasseur pushed on the door. It didn't budge. Bernie stepped over and assisted, using his shoulder. The door groaned open and stirred up a plume of dust from the stair landing. Father Lavasseur stepped back quickly to avoid soiling his white robe.

The open door shed light on the small landing with stairs leading down sideways and to the left along the basement foundation. Father Lavasseur flipped up the light switch and they all looked up at the empty socket.

"Someone was apparently desperate for a light bulb," Father Lavasseur said with a chuckle.

Bernie got out his phone and turned on his flashlight. Lilly did the same.

"I'll wait here for you, if you don't mind, the dust is offensive to my robe."

"Not at all," Bernie replied, stepping onto the landing, then motioned to Lilly. They pointed their lights down the stairs. At the bottom, a cinder block propped open a door leading into a darkened room.

"Ready?" Bernie asked?

Lilly nodded and tried to smile, then followed Bernie down the stairs.

"Please hold on to the railing," Father Lavasseur cautioned them. "And do not disrupt anything, s'il vous plait. I hope you find a light that functions down there."

"Okay, thanks," Bernie yelled up the stairs, as they entered the darkened room. Bernie groped for a light switch, found one, and flipped it up. A shop light sputtered to life hanging over a dirty work bench standing along the rear wall. One of two fluorescent bulbs struggled to illuminate a set of empty shelves against the left wall. A lawn mower frame missing its engine, handle and wheels leaned abandoned against the right wall. Cobwebs hung from the low ceiling with new versions spun thick in every corner. The floor consisted of square, cut stones covered in a thick layer of dirt, and coal dust that rose with each foot fall.

"We have a light that works!" Bernie hollered up the stairs.

"Good to hear," Father Lavasseur responded. "Take your time."

"Doesn't look like anyone's been down here in a while," Lilly said, as they explored the dingy room, making fresh footprints on the floor.

Bernie picked up the lawn mower frame, said, "This must be from the seventies." He leaned the frame back against the wall, then bent down to look at a ripped page from a newspaper.

"Find something?" Lilly asked, sounding hopeful.

"It's just a partial page from a French newspaper. The header part is missing. I was hoping to find a date." He tossed the paper back on the floor and scooped up a handful of the flour-like detritus, said, "Definitely looks like this was used to store heating fuels back in the day." He held his palm up with a small pile of the floor's contents for Lilly to see.

"Yeah, lots of black specks," she replied.

Bernie stood up, tipped his hand, and watched the fine mixture trickle down. Noticing what looked like a carved pattern on a stone's surface, he kneeled and brushed off the remaining debris with his hand, said, "Hey babe, look at this."

Lilly walked over and saw the pattern etched into the face of the stone. The carved relief looked rudimentary and impressionistic.

"Is that a bull?" she asked, sounding surprised.

"Yeah, looks like horns there," he replied, tracing the outline with his finger. "Hand carved stones in a coal room? Why would they do that?"

"Wow, that does seem odd, but it's very cool," Lilly said, as she kneeled to get a closer look, then slid her finger along the grooves.

Bernie found a flattened paper cup to help scrape dirt off adjacent stones while Lilly held out her phone light for him, but none held an image. The fourth stone over revealed the etched likeness of a snake or perhaps a river, they couldn't decide.

Doubling their efforts, Lilly found a torn rag to clear debris from stones and soon found the likeness of a horse. Then, Bernie uncovered a lion, Lilly, a bird. They called out the names of each newly discovered image.

"Look, Bernie, this must be an elephant."

"Are you two doing okay down there?" They heard Father Lavasseur call from the top of the stairs.

"Shoot, I forgot about Father Lavasseur," Bernie said.

"Oh, no, I did too."

"I'll go talk to him," Bernie said, then he ran up the stairs to the sidewalk.

"I apologize," Bernie said, sounding slightly out of breath, dust patched his clothes and hands. "We found carvings on some of the floor stones and lost track of time."

Father Lavasseur looked surprised and asked, "Carvings of what?"

"Mostly animals and things from nature, like a lion, a bird, and a river," Bernie replied and scratched his head. Then, thinking out loud, added enthusiastically, "The room looks about ten feet by ten feet, so I'd guess there's about a hundred stones to brush off, but not all have an image, and some are under the workbench. I'd like to document what we find if you'd allow us to."

Father Levasseur's left eye squinted, and he replied in a tone of concern, "I'm sorry but I need to go back inside. I have a meeting with a young couple concerning their betrothal." Bernie pleaded his case, "Perhaps we can come back this afternoon?"

Father Lavasseur looked at the open door, then at Bernie and replied in a compassionate tone, "Look, I see no harm in leaving you two on your own for a while. I'm curious why my predecessors put in that effort for the floor of a heating fuel room."

"Oh, thank you father, and I agree. We'll take pictures and share what we find."

"Sure, of course, just be careful down there," Father Lavasseur cautioned as he removed the door's key from his keyring and handed it to Bernie. "Turn out the light and secure both locks. I'll meet you near the altar. Ask for me and I'll come out when I can."

Bernie pocketed the key, thanked the father excessively, then rushed back down to hunt for images.

Bernie and Lilly worked their way across and down in a grid pattern. Fine dust coated their arms and legs. Lilly swept off a stone under the lower shelf of the work bench when her phone's screen flashed a low battery warning.

"Oh no, my phone's going dead. I forgot to charge it last night." She turned off the light and pocketed her phone.

"Darn," Bernie replied. "I still have sixty-eight percent. We can share. Holler when you need it."

"Okay."

"Finding any stones with words or names?" Bernie asked.

"Not yet, just images. I'm having a little trouble getting to the stones under the workbench. There's not a lot of clearance with this lower shelf."

Bernie eyed the heavy looking wood bench, replied, "It's not going anywhere. Looks like we'll have to skip the last couple rows underneath."

"Yep, I'm working on the last row we can get to."

Resuming her work, Lilly revealed a series of lines coming from what looked like a round circle in the center of the stone.

"Hey Bern, will you bring your light over for a minute?"

"Sure. What'd you find?"

"Not quite sure yet," she replied, abandoning the rag to brush off the remaining dirt with her hand. Impulsively, she jerked away, bumping her knuckles on the shelf.

"Ouch!" she cried.

"What the heck? Did you get bit by a spider?" Bernie asked. "No, that stone feels warm," Lilly said. "It just surprised me, and I hit my knuckles. Feel it."

Bernie examined her slightly reddened knuckles.

"I meant feel the stone, not my hand."

"You probably just created friction brushing off the surface."

"That wasn't just friction," Lilly countered.

Bernie kissed Lilly's knuckles, then leaned in and placed his hand on the cleared stone. His expression changed to inspired wonder, said, "Huh, this one is a little bit warm."
Bernie brushed off surrounding stones and felt each one. His left eyebrow shot up. He looked at Lilly, said, "These others are not warm."

"What do you think's causing the heat?" she asked.

"Must be a buried steam pipe or possibly an electric utility," Bernie replied. "But this room must be way older than either of those technologies, so that doesn't add up." He felt the tops of neighboring stones again. "Did you figure out what the carving is?"

"Not yet, it's too dim." Lilly replied. Bernie held his phone light for her. With mild trepidation, she reached down and felt the stone's warmth, then ran her fingers along the etched lines to the round center. An inspired look crossed her face, she said, "I think it's the sun."

"Lilly, you're right. And it links to the poem's last line, her warm sun's rays."

"Oh, Bernie, we found another clue! What do you think it means?"

"Not sure, but there must be something underneath. Let's take the rock out. I need something to dig with." Bernie got up to look around. "Here we go." He picked up a six-inch-long shaft of a screwdriver, its handle missing.

Lilly, shaking with excitement, concentrated on holding Bernie's phone light steady while he scraped dirt from the cracks, then pried the stone loose. He slid it forward and out and set it aside. They peered into the hole but saw only dirt.

Bernie used the metal shaft to gently probe and loosen the compacted soil. Concerned he might accidentally puncture something, he swung his legs around to change position, said, "I wish this damn shelf wasn't here."

"Tell me about it," Lilly quipped, as she glanced at her reddened knuckles.

Despite the slow-going, they eventually heard a scraping sound like metal on metal. Bernie put the screwdriver shaft aside and used his bare hands to probe the dirt.

"It's something flat, so it's not a pipe," he said, then scooped out the dirt.

Gazing in, they saw rusty metal just smaller than the stone-sized hole. Bernie said, "It must be the top or a lid to something, maybe be an electrical box. If we remove the stone in front, then dig down, we can see how deep it is."

"Bernie," Lilly said with a voice of caution, "Father Lavasseur said not to disturb anything and we're already digging up his floor."

Bernie looked at the hole, then at the pile of dirt next to a centuries-old displaced etched stone conveying the image of the sun. He remembered his vows to behave, looked at Lilly and said, "You're right. Maybe we should go ask him first and tell him what we've found so far. Tell him we're digging up his basement. I'm sure he won't mind."

They stood up and looked at each other in confused silence, a serious mood stirred the room with the drifting dust.

Bernie said, "I mean, whatever's down there might be dangerous. What if it is an electrical box and I puncture it? You...we might get hurt, maybe even arrested again for destruction of property."

Lilly responded, "So, we'll end up in a hospital first and then go to prison?"

"Yes."

"Well in that case, let's go ask for a shovel."

"You know," Bernie said thoughtfully, "If it is a safety hazard causing the heat we should seriously investigate and report what we find to Father Levasseur."

Lilly looked at Bernie with consternation, asked, "Will you be super careful?"

"Cross my heart, we'll just take a quick look."

"Okay, but only for the sake of safety."

"Exactly."

Clear of the workbench, the imageless front stone came up easily. Bernie set it aside, then cautiously probed the dirt with the screwdriver shaft finding only soft, sandy soil. Working together, they quickly scooped out the dirt, revealing the front edges of a metal box.

Bernie said, "Looks like it's about six inches deep. I don't think it's a utility."

"What's causing the heat, then?" Lilly asked, feeling the exposed edge of the rusty box.

"That's the million-dollar question," Bernie replied. "I'm surprised no one's dug it up yet."

"You wouldn't think anything about it unless you touched that one stone."

Bernie asked, "So, do we stop here and put everything back?"

"That was the plan, but maybe we should look inside the box, I mean, it's right here in front of us."

Bernie stopped and looked Lilly firmly in the eyes, replied, "I seem to always get myself in trouble and I don't want to drag you down with me this time."

"Bernie, something important must be in there, and it's not a coincidence we're here. We just found what Moridorno wanted us to find. Cecilia's love for Aditya could not absolve his sin. She patiently guards his warm sun's rays. Moridorno must have etched these stones."

Bernie looked at the stone with the sun and shook his head, then sat back on his butt, not caring about the dirt, his arms hung over his knees. He bowed his head between them and looked defeated.

"Bern, are you okay?"

Bernie lifted his head and chuckled, said, "You're right, we've been through a lot to get here."

"What's funny?"

"I'm just wondering who Moridorno imagined might find this box. What are the odds it would be us?" Bernie got up and made a futile effort to brush off his pants, creating a small plume. He said, "Okay, let's just take a quick look, then we put it all back."

Lilly's face lit up. "Deal."

To avoid damage, Bernie worked at a careful pace. With most of the dirt cleared away, he slowly pulled out the box from the front, stood up and placed it on the work bench. Corrosion covered most of the exterior and the corner braces had peeled back in places.

"It's in rough shape, but still holding," he said. "It looks like hammered steel with the sides pounded over in places to hold the lid on." He used the screwdriver shaft to peel back the corroding steel and easily worked the lid free, revealing a cloth with outlines of something inside.

Bernie lifted the object, said, "It feels like books. They're warm, feel." He held the bundle out for Lilly.

She took a step back with a concerned look, asked, "No, Bernie, what if it's radioactive or something? Your hand is going to melt, and you'll get cancer."

Bernie's expression turned serious, and he quickly put the package back in the box, said,

"That's a good point, except Madame Currie didn't discover radium until 1902, so I'm pretty sure it's not possible." Bernie examined his hands, turning them over, then held them out for Lilly. "See? They look and feel normal." Bernie picked up the package again and unfurled the cloth revealing two books: a tall, thin black book, and a thicker one with smaller dimensions. "These books aren't causing the heat. There must be something underneath them." Bernie looked at Lilly's furrowed brow lines, asked, "Do you want me to continue?"

Lilly stared at the box, said, "Let's look at the books first."

Bernie opened the smaller, thicker book with a beige cloth cover and carefully looked through the pages, he said, "Looks like lots of drawings of plants. And what language is this?"

Lilly replied, "It's not Italian. Looks Arabic, maybe?"

"Possibly."

Bernie picked up the other book and examined the plain black cover made from what appeared to be animal hide with a hand sewn inner black cloth lining. The inner handmade pages felt thick and firm with foreign writing flourished by the tip of a quill pen.

Bernie examined the first page, and said, "It looks like a map. Maybe Old Europe with some of Asia and Russia up here, see the faded lines and dots?"

"I do," Lilly replied. "This looks like a version from shortly after the reign of Genghis Khan." She adjusted the angle of Bernie's phone light. "The writing looks like Italian and probably names cities or regions of that time.

Bernie meticulously pulled apart the next page revealing a large, flourished header.

"I'll translate that," Lilly volunteered as she tapped on her phone app, "The header says, our holy order."

Under the header, in faded writing, the page held fifteen names with dates and locations. The first name listed Father De La Croix, 1040 - 1095.

"Whoa," Bernie said, sounding amazed. "Ten-forty? That's a while ago."

"Look, our friends!" Lilly exclaimed, pointing. "There's Eufrasio Fionscetti listed third, and Despachal Moridorno, the final name on the list, fifteen eighty-two, same year he wrote the letter."

Bernie teased apart the next pages, said, "Looks like there's only three pages, but lots of writing on this last one."

Lilly replied, "Yeah, that one needs some translating, but before we do that, let's see what else is in the box that's causing the heat."

Bernie said, "Okay, let's do." He brushed off a section of the work bench and put down the books, then reached in the box and pulled out a layer of what looked like thick grey lamb's wool and set the wad on the workbench next to the books.

"Must be for insulation," Bernie suggested.

Peering inside the box, nested in more wool, they saw a piece of silver colored metal about two inches thick, slightly larger than Bernie's hand. Lilly held the light closer as he picked up the object.

"Careful," she cautioned.

"It's really warm," Bernie said, as he turned the metal over in his hands. "It's not very heavy." One end looked smooth and rounded with some scratches, the other looked jagged with torn edges.

"So, what's producing the heat?" Lilly asked.

"I have no idea," Bernie said. "Looks like it hit something and broke off from something else. He placed the metal back in its woolen nest.

"Let's take another look at the black book," Lilly suggested as she delicately opened it. "The books are in good shape."

Bernie replied, "The heat must have kept the moisture level low."

Lilly tapped on her phone app and said, "The page says something about a sacred historic order." Tap-tap-tap. "Entrusted knowledge and God's warmth sent from heaven." Tap-tap-tap. "Overcoming persecution. There's more, but..."

"Moridorno had to hide it," Bernie interrupted. "And he left clues for someone...for us to find."

"And he hid it in a cathedral built for the persecution of heretics," Lilly added as she giggled at the irony.

Bernie stared at the mysterious metal nested in its wool and said thoughtfully, "I wonder how far back the history of this metal goes. I mean, how long has this been passed through time?"

"At least back to Father De La Croix from the eleventh century," Lilly replied.

"Makes me wonder when and where this metal came from maybe before these guys formed their historic order."

"All good points," Lilly said, then her expression changed, she asked, "Remember Moridorno's closing line from his original letter?"

"I do," Bernie replied. "Allied forever in all things holy on earth and those from heaven." "Correct, but don't most preachers say those in heaven, not from heaven?" Bernie opened his mouth to answer, but Lilly continued, "And a similar line from this black book, God's warmth sent from heaven, could mean the metal came from aliens and this broke off their spaceship," Lilly proposed in a serious tone, her face stoic as she looked at Bernie, who momentarily returned her demeanor. The dim light cast shadows over the contours of their dusty faces as they stared at each other in silence, then cracked simultaneous grins, that broke into full-on smiles.

Bernie teased, "Quick, check the stairs, they might be coming back for their missing part." His jovial tone shed nervous energy as the pair stared at each other, searching for a rational thought.

Lilly, finding her voice of reason, said, "Bernie, these books alone must be worth a fortune, and I'm not quite sure what to think about the metal, but it's not your everyday common steel. By the way, how are your hands?" He held them out, said, "They feel normal. They're not turning red."

"But we can't sell any of this," Bernie concluded as he ran a grimy hand through his hair. "We need to put it all back."

"What? But Bernie, we've come all this way. Moridorno wanted someone to find this. Plus, looking at the bigger picture here, it's massively historic."

"It's not ours, "Bernie countered. "And we can't just steal it. Remember my vow? Now it seems you want to break through a proverbial fence."

"Okay, you are right in that respect. So, do we go tell Father Lavasseur?"

"I'm pretty sure we should not go say, 'Hey man, we just dug up your basement like you told us not to and found some space junk that apparently produces some form of perpetual energy. And, oh yeah, this comes with a couple old books, one that lists a dozen priests who served in this very cathedral and knew about the metal thing since at least the eleventh century."

They stared at each other, absorbing the absurdity of what Bernie just laid out. Lilly replied, "Well, when you put it that way."

After a few moments of thought, Bernie's left eyebrow shot up. He said, "Right now I'm thinking we take pictures of everything, put this all back, and tell no one. We'll go home and research what's in the books and find out what the metal thing might be."

"Do we tell Attuchi?" Lilly asked.

"We probably should eventually, but for now, we better keep this strictly between the two of us."

"Okay, I agree," Lilly replied.

Bernie checked his phone for the time, said, "Yikes, it's twenty to one already, we've been down here a while. We better finish up. I'll take pictures of each page of the black book, and a few of the botanical book, then get some shots of the box and metal thing while you brush off the last few stones that have images. Then while I re-bury the box, you can use my phone to snap pictures of the floor. We can lay out a grid pattern when we get back home."

"Sounds good."

They got to work.

Satisfied with their photography, Bernie resealed the box and eased it into the hole, tamped down the backfilled dirt, leveled the top with the screwdriver shaft and placed the stones back on top. Next, he pushed dirt between the cracks, then stood up to inspect his work. Not quite satisfied, he scooped up a handful of dirt and sprinkled the silt over the two stones, then brushed them off to match the others.

They walked to the doorway and took a final look around at Bernie's repair work and the small mounds of dirt patterned across the floor. He flipped off the light and they rushed up the stairs to the sidewalk and fresh air. Bernie felt shocked at how dirty Lilly looked in the daylight as she shook out her hair and combed her fingers through it. As they patted and brushed themselves off,

plumes of silty dirt and coal dust spread in the breeze.

"That's good enough," Bernie said urgently, and quickly relocked both deadbolts; then they ran toward the front entrance.

"How do your hands feel?" Lilly asked as they neared the front doors.

Bernie held them up and rotated them, said, "The look filthy, but feel normal."

They rushed inside and walked briskly to the front, avoiding patrons since they looked like tramps. In the front right pew, Father Lavasseur sat patiently reading from a small stack of papers. When Bernie and Lilly stopped in front of him, he looked up with surprise, then disgust.

"Sorry we took so long," Bernie said, sounding winded.

"And so dirty," Lilly added apologetically.

"That's quite alright, Father Lavasseur replied. "I'm just going over tomorrow's sermon. Let's talk over here." Father Lavasseur stood up and motioned to a side corridor.

He unclipped the rope barrier and they walked a short distance down the dimly lit hallway. Bernie handed the key to Father Lavasseur who got out his key ring and began slipping it back on. He said, "My, you two certainly take your work seriously. Did you find more images?"

"Yes, we found quite a few," Bernie replied enthusiastically and got out his phone to share the pictures, taking care not to scroll to the metal box.

Father Lavasseur looked on with interest, said, "I had no idea these were down there. Look here, is that a fish?"

Bernie zoomed in a little. Lilly leaned in to look, said, "Yes, that's right. We discovered fifteen images, but there's probably a few more under the work bench."

"Ah, that's right," Father Lavasseur said. "That sturdy old work bench. Well, thank you for sharing those pictures, and for all the work you've done."

"You are most welcome," Bernie replied. "Thank you for allowing us to look around."

"You are most welcome. It appears you'll be taking some of Saint Cecilia's dirt with you," Father Lavasseur said with a grin. They laughed, but Father Lavasseur, with his years of working with people, sensed a nervousness with the young women, something seemed off.

"Very true," Bernie agreed. "We need a shower and a change of clothes. Thank you again for your gracious hospitality. I'll email you these pictures and we'll map out the carvings after we get back home."

"I would be appreciative and fascinated by such a gesture. Do you have further plans for your stay in Albi? Perhaps you can come to our service tomorrow morning? It would be an honor."

"Thank you for the offer, Father Lavasseur, but we fly out in the morning," Lilly answered. "And like Bernie said, we'll try to determine if there's a story or a pattern in the carved images." She glanced from Father Lavasseur to Bernie, then looked at the floor. Father Lavasseur again sensed something odd about the young woman's body language.

"Do you have a card or something with your contact information?" Bernie asked.

"Yes, I do," Father Lavasseur replied as he broke from his conspiratorial thoughts. He reached inside his robe to a breast pocket and pulled out a card and handed it to Bernie. After a final round of good-byes, the dusty couple walked briskly to their rental car. Driving away, Bernie watched the church shrink in the rear-view mirror, then looked again closely at his hands.

In his office, Father Lavasseur took off his church garb, then walked to the coal room, unlocked the door, and walked down the dusty stairs. The dim light over the workbench sputtered to life. He stepped between the dirt piles and kneeled to examine several carvings, then stood at the workbench and saw a square imprint in the dust next to a brushed off area that contained grey fibers, crumbs of rich soil, and flakes of rust. He looked at the lawn mower frame and tilted his head like a curious dog.

Standing at the door, a finger on the light switch, he took one last look around. A trickle of sweat ran down his neck, then tickled his back. He clicked off the light and walked up the stairs.

Chapter 22

Back in the USA

Bernie leaned over Lilly to see out the jet's window at the verdant hills of West Virginia spreading to the horizon like flowing water in a giant stream.

"I hope you don't mind," Bernie said. "I just love this perspective as we come in for a landing."

Lilly rubbed his back and replied, "Not at all. Thanks for giving me the window seat most of the time."

On the drive to their condo, Bernie checked his rear-view mirror often, a habit formed out of necessary paranoia. When a vehicle turned with them, he noticed the color and model and tracked how long they followed.

"Can someone feel thrilled and petrified at the same time?" Lilly asked.

"I feel that way sometimes, especially with the information we now possess," Bernie replied. "It doesn't seem real. I mean, why us?"

After two days of recuperation from jet lag, they fully unpacked and got laundry washed, folded, and put away. Then Bernie made restocking the store a priority and attended several successful sales events. Lilly priced antiques in the back room as fast as she could to fill in the empty spots on the shelves. To end the hectic work week, Bernie's parents invited the couple out for dinner.

On Friday at six-thirty, they met at one of Chris' favorite restaurants. Their server dropped off drinks and got main entrees ordered. Bryson took a swig of his Manhattan, then turned to his son and Lilly, said, "So tell us about your recent adventures in France."

Bernie and Lilly exchanged glances, figuring out who should start.

Bernie nodded.

Lilly cleared her throat, said, "Okay, it was better than usual. We had a really good time and took a little side trip to Agde on the Mediterranean Sea."

Bernie interrupted, "We went parasailing behind a boat! Sorry, go ahead."

Lilly continued, "It was scary at first, but once we got used to it, the views were awesome."

"You kids sure know how to have fun," Chris said with a large smile.

Lilly continued, "After that, back in Albi, at Saint Cecilia's Cathedral, we met Father Lavasseur, who gave us a tour. We ended up finding some unique hand carved floor stones in a small basement room." She paused and gave Bernie an inquisitive look.

Chris noticed the shared facial expressions. *Something about the basement room is special,* she reasoned, as a mother who instilled her son's mannerisms.

Bernie picked up the story, "The stones are about one foot square, and the room is about ten feet by ten feet. The room was last used last as a maintenance room. Before that it stored wood, then coal."

"So, you found a hundred hand carved tiles?" Bryson asked.

Bernie replied, "No, only fifteen had carvings. There's a workbench covering the back couple rows, so there are probably a few more stones that have carvings. We took pictures and documented the images."

Lilly added, "We've been so busy at the store, we haven't done any research on them yet. Your son has been buying a lot of antiques, lately."

"But the store looks good again," Bernie said, smiling proudly.

The following Tuesday, Bernie and Lilly stayed busy working at the store during the morning but took the rest of the afternoon off to examine the pictures of the books. In the privacy of their condo and after a couple sandwiches, Bernie poured wine, got out his phone and mirrored his pictures on the tv, then scanned through the botanical pictures. He asked Lilly, "Do you know anything about plants and their medicinal purposes?"

"Not really, just that Aloe Vera is good for burns. We should compare these with online pictures or maybe go to the library."

Bernie swiped to the next picture from the botanical book, asked, "What language is that?"

"I'm pretty sure I have no idea," Lilly replied.

"Okay, I'll send a couple photos of the plant book to Sean. Maybe he can ask someone in the botanical sciences department and find out what these are and then ask the linguistics department to figure out what language this is."

"Good idea. It's awesome you have a friend at the U."

"Yeah, Sean likes this kind of stuff." Bernie scrolled to pictures of pages from the black book.

Lilly said, "There's the map of Old Europe." She opened her laptop and pulled up maps from the fifteen hundreds.

Bernie said, "Look, here's a faint dotted line leading from Florence, Italy to Albi, France to Budapest, then Russia and back to Albi. He swiped his finger to the next picture. Page two contained a column of names listing each member of the Holy Order, followed by dates:

Father Demetri Delacroix	1040-1095	Santa Maria
Father Nicoli Fiore	1096-1119	Santa Maria
Father Eufrasio Fionscetti	1120-1157	Santa Maria
Father Andre Petrov	1158-1181	Basilica de San Lorenzo
Father Pierre Simone	1182-1224	Basílica de San Lorenzo
Father Carlos Ricotti	1225-1272	Saint Cecelia
Father Gianni Mansueto	1273-1326	Saint Cecelia
Father Ettore Calimero	1327-1354	Lady de Trier
Father Ugo Oreste	1355-1387	Lady de Trier
Father Alfonse Emerson	1388-1411	Lady de Trier
Father Horatio Sugaftor	1412-1441	Notre Dame
Father Magus Vita	1442-1473	Saint Cecelia
Father Theon Arram	1474-1516	Saint Cecelia
Father Remus Cieus	1517-1556	Saint Cecelia
Father Despachal Moridorno	1557 -1582	Saint Cecelia

Lilly said solemnly, "The secret of the metal has been kept by all these men at all these places for so many years."

"It's astounding," Bernie replied. "Records began at the Santa Maria. Where is that?"

Lilly looked it up, said, "Florence, Italy. Not too surprising."

"And the Basilica de San Lorenzo?"

"In Florence, as well," Lilly replied. "Just switched to a different church."

"In thirteen thirty-seven, the metal got moved to Lady de Trier. Where is that?"

Lilly tapped on her keyboard and replied, "Trier, Rhineland Palatinate, Germany. Maybe they moved it during the worst part of the hundred years war."

"Good point. They didn't want it to fall into British hands."

Lilly said, "It's even been in Notre Dame for a short while."

"How cool is that?" Bernie swiped to the next picture, zoomed in, and said, "Page three has a lot of information. How about if I translate and you take notes?"

"Sounds good."

Bernie booted up his laptop and tapped on his keys.

Lilly got out a pen and notebook, said, "Ready."

Bernie's left eyebrow shot up as he read haltingly, "It starts out, to whomever reads this, you have followed a path to enlightenment. I feared losing this factum with gifts from a higher power forever buried in a dreary cellar. Its magic comes from a place beyond the horizon while it's strange warmth echoes through the centuries, yet the bible makes no mention. I and my former clergy struggled with its mystic power. Some felt the metal possessed demonic Luciferic ties and called for it to be cast into the sea. My predecessor decided to bury the mercurial oddity, Satan's metal, he called it. He chose to end its legacy, to allow its knowledge of existence to die, buried in the dreary cellar. I felt guilt and remorse, so I dug it up.

I felt it somehow held ties to God. I allowed only two dear friends and fellow priests, Ansel and Valdemar, to know of the metal. They helped me carve images on the basement flag stones to complete the riddle. With permission from the Ansel family, I hired the inscription for his tombstone when I traveled to Donaueschingen to preside over his funeral. As I progressed in age, I fashioned a box, and added the two books. One with a map of my travels and a list of priests who had carried on our secret. Another contains plant and herbal remedies passed down through the ages. I purchased the book many years ago during my travels but can't recall which city.

Using my last breath, my last thought, I will rest with my sin and pray mankind someday finds his Eden. Here in lies my secret, resting under her warm sun's rays." Bernie stopped reading and looked at Lilly.

"Wow, I'm speechless," she said. "They kept the metal from the public for centuries. This is some crazy insight."

"And now we know," Bernie said, sounding a bit mystified. "I kind of feel like we have a responsibility to find out what causes the heat. It could benefit all mankind, just like Moridorno's art."

Lilly replied, "I think Father Moridorno would want that, especially now, with our current technology. So do we tell Father Lavasseur about it?" Lilly asked.

"Hmm," Bernie replied. "If we did, he would probably feel obligated to report it, and we'll never get anywhere near that room again."

"So, what's next? Go back and smuggle it out?"

"Sure, Lilly, you make it sound so simple. On one hand, it's criminally wrong, so right up my alley, check off that box. But on the other hand, do we have a moral obligation to share a sample of perpetual energy for the good of history and science?"

"But we can't be sure it's safe," Lilly countered. "Our exposure was only a few minutes."

"True, I suppose it could be harmful with a longer exposure," Bernie replied, then chuckled.

"What's funny?"

"The irony that doing the wrong illegal thing might, in the bigger picture, turn out to be the right thing to do."

"I agree," Lilly said as the pair stared at each other in thought, searching for the correct answer.

Bernie spoke up, "If we go back, there are several issues to consider why we can't go public with this knowledge, assuming everything goes well."

"Oh, what else is there?"

"First, like I said, Father Lavasseur will figure things out and be obligated to report the metal and books stolen. We could have arrest warrants out against us, with possible extradition to France. Second, we signed a contract to disclose and turn over anything we find to Attuchi for his client, so legally we couldn't keep anything. Third, Beufort and his henchmen will be on us again. They may even know about the metal and are just waiting for us to lead them to it."

"Wow, you lay it on thick, don't you? It's not so simple."

"I wish it were. But before we do anything else, we need to sit down and diagram the images in coal room for Father Lavasseur."

The following morning, Shandra felt sick and couldn't work, and Seth had the day off. With Katy scheduled at noon, Bernie and Lilly needed to open the store by nine. They got up early to stop at a mud hut for lattes on the way to the silo and enjoyed their rich creaminess in the seating area by seven-twenty.

Lilly said, "I saw in Shandra's text it's just a cold, so she should be back to work tomorrow."

"Yeah, that's the good news," Bernie replied. "We have an hour before we should head over to open the store." He got out his phone and scanned to the coal room photos, said, "Here we are." Lilly leaned in.

They examined the various photos taken from different angles of the carved stones in relationship to the room. Lilly got out her note pad and made a grid that noted the placement of the workbench and each carved stone.

Then, Lilly added a few notes:

The work bench obscures column eight partially, and fully obscures columns 9 and 10. Based on the number of observable carved stones, we estimate 3 or 4 more etched stones are under the work bench for a total of 18 or 19 in total.

"Okay, that's a good start," she said.

"I agree. Father Lavasseur will appreciate knowing the layout."

As Lilly packed up, getting ready to head to the store, she paused, said, "I have an idea, how about if we take this a step further and include biblical passages that relate to the images."

"I like it."

Bernie and Lilly walked to the store, turned on the lights and set up the cash register. At eight fifty-five, Lilly turned on the open sign. With no early-bird customers, the pair looked up relatable biblical passages for each image. Bernie listed them in a Word document on his laptop:

Horse - *Psalms 32:9 - Do not be like the horse or the mule, which have no understanding but must be controlled by bit and bridle or they will not come to you.*

Snail - *Psalms 58:8 - Which thrusts forth itself, and seems to threaten with its horns, but is quickly dissolved. For it wastes by its own motions, in every stretch it makes, leaving some of its moisture behind, which, by degrees, must needs consume it, though it makes a path to shine after it.*

Lion - *1 Peter 5:8 - Be sober, be watchful: your adversary the devil, as a roaring lion, walketh about, seeking whom he may devour.*

Bird - *Psalms 50:11 - I know all the fowls of the mountains God not only knows them but takes care of them; not a sparrow falls to the ground without his knowledge, and all the fowls of the air are fed by him.*

Elephant - *A symbol of patience, chastity, and temperance.*

Fish - *Matthew 4:19 - And he saith unto them, follow me, and I will make you fishers of men.*

Bull - *Associated with strength and fertility.*

Bear - *Proverbs 17:12 - It is better to meet a bear robbed of her whelps, than a fool trusting in his own folly.*

River - *Flowing water reflects the history of humanity.*

Goat - *Hebrews 10:4 - It is impossible the blood of goats should take away sins, either the guilt or the power of them.*

Sun - *Isaiah 9:2 - The people who walk in darkness will see a great light. For those who live in a land of deep darkness, a light will shine.*

Rat - *Leviticus 11:29 - These also shall be unclean unto you among the creeping things that creep upon the earth, the weasel, and the mouse, and the tortoise after his kind.*

Rooster - *A symbol of vigilance and faithfulness.*

Locust - Matthew 3:4 - *Now John wore a garment of camel's hair and a leather belt around his waist, and his food was locusts and wild honey.*

Spider - Isaiah 59:5 - *They hatch deadly snakes and weave spiders' webs. Whoever eats their eggs will die; whoever cracks them will hatch a viper.*

"I think Father Lavasseur will like our extra effort," Lilly said.

"I agree," Bernie said as he snapped a photo of Lilly's neatly drawn coal room diagram. "So, I'll email this diagram and the biblical references in a while. What else should we tell him?"

An unsettled feeling hung in the air. Lilly replied, "Are we ever going back?"

The couple locked eyes, trying to stay afloat of their turbulent thoughts.

Bernie replied, "We probably shouldn't, considering that laundry list I just read of reasons not to."

"What if we just go back for the books? You know, it's our responsibility for the sake of history. We can leave the weird metal thing. I still think it might be dangerous."

Bernie's facial expressions turned a blend of shock and intrigue, he asked, "I know it's tempting to go back, but I prefer to stay out of jail."

"We wouldn't have to tell anyone."

"It's still wrong and you shouldn't be tempting me like this."

"The metal might survive, but the box will corrode and then the books will eventually rot. And here's another reason we should go back, maybe for the metal too. Anyone can trace where we've been. I've seen you use your credit card most of the time during our travels. Beufort already knows exactly where we've been since he's been following us. Anyone who knows about Moridorno's letter could figure out the clues just like we did and it's going to lead them to Saint Cecelia's. If Father Lavasseur puts two and two together, he will show them the coal room and they'll find the stone with her warm sun's rays. Well, then the cat's out of the sack. The metal's out of the box. The books are…"

"Okay, enough!" Bernie interrupted. That was quite a shot-gun blast of rebuttal. I hadn't considered anyone duplicating what we did. That is concerning."

"Someone from Beufort's team might be at Saint Cecelia's right now pulling up stones in the coal room."

"Stop. Okay, maybe we should go back, but before we decide, let's see what Sean finds out about the photos."

"You have a deal."

After a few days of witnessing time crawl by, Bernie sat at his desk in his silo office entering accounts payable when he heard a ping indicating the much-anticipated email from Sean. He clicked it open and read,

Hi Bernie,

Sorry for the delayed response, but I've been swamped with grading papers. Why do I assign those? lol So, the pictures you sent are extremely unique. The botanist told me the plants are of unknow origin. Where the hell did you get this? My associate in the language department claims what you have, share characteristics similar to the Voynich Manuscript, named after Wilfred M. Voynich, a book dealer who acquired the rare manuscript in 1912. The book is a codex filled with drawings of strange plants and undetermined writing. I'm sure you'll investigate further, but some historians claim it's someone's medicinal plant catalogue hidden in the codex to protect them from accusations of witchcraft. Others claim it's a hoax and the writing is gibberish, similar to the fanciful speculation the manuscript has an alien origin. (Will I see this in the tabloids soon? lol)

Per your request, the botanist and linguistic professors vowed not to tell anyone about your book, but if you go public with this find, they would love to examine the original and be a part of any publications. It sounds like a big deal! If you have a similar copy of a Voynich Manuscript, you, my friend, hit the jackpot once again. I did a quick online query and found it's basically priceless, but if it were to go to auction, it could fetch between 50 and 100 million. Maybe I should have been an antiques dealer!?!? Lol (Where do I apply????)

When are we going out for beers? You owe me one or two – and it sure seems like you can afford a couple rounds!

Cheers!
Sean

Bernie forwarded Sean's email to Lilly, with 'This Sweetens the Pot' in the subject line. He finished his office work and walked over to the store. He chatted briefly with Shandra at the front counter, then found Lilly leaning over her workstation in the back room, her laptop open.

"Hi Lilly."

"Hey, I just read Sean's email."

"Pretty weird, huh?"

"I'll say. He mentioned alien origin. I read that part twice. Bernie, what did we find in that church basement?"

"I'm sure we'll find that it's quite earthly. Although, I sent Sean a follow up email to make sure he and his associates don't share this information."

"Good call," Lilly replied. "And you're right, the deal just got sweeter!"

Later that afternoon, Bernie attached the coal room diagram and biblical passages in an email, then typed:

Dear Father Lavasseur,

I'd like to thank you again for the hospitality you showed us during our recent visit to your cathedral. As promised, please find two attachments that include a rough diagram showing the arrangement of the carved images on the coal room's floor.

For the second attachment, Lilly and I took a leap of faith, and looked up some possible biblical verses that may somehow relate with the images. So far, we haven't found any clues that lead us anywhere further.

If it's alright, Lilly and I would like to make another visit to Albi in the near future. We would like to visit you and your wonderful cathedral and, in the coal room, make impressions of the stones using tracing paper. Plus, using mirrors, we can get a look at the stones under the work bench. (We assume that the workbench is a fairly recent addition to the room.) Lilly has proposed writing a publishable article, perhaps even a book about the carved images and the history of the coal room. Any input from your perspective would be greatly appreciated.

Lastly, and I don't know how to put this delicately, but from what we saw during our last visit, you may experience resistance from Monsignor Dubaux, so perhaps we can align our visit when he's away again, that is, if you will allow it.

Sincerely, and for the good of theological history,
Bernard Maynard

He pushed send and sat back in his office chair and considered the six-hour time zone change. *In Albi, it's 3:30 in the afternoon. I doubt he'll reply today.*

Bernie was right, but the following morning, sitting up in bed, he opened his email, he tapped Lilly to wake her and said, "He replied." Lilly sat up and leaned over, they read,

Dearest Bernie and Lilly,

My heart swells to hear you take such an interest in God's work. I applaud your biblical references to the carved stones, and to learn of the specific varieties you found. I had no idea they were there. Thank you for sending these. Before I sat down to reply to your letter, I felt hesitant to allow you another visit, since I found little reason for anyone to investigate the carved stones any further. But, after deeper thought and prayer, I find little harm in it. However, we would need to get permission to allow any publications. I think if you two shed our glorious lady in a positive *way, this may be a good source to promote Saint Cecelia's Cathedral and the Lord's path.*

So, you may come at your convenience. Sadly, Monsignor Dubaux had heart surgery about two weeks ago, so he will be absent for a few months. I am in charge during his recovery and will grant you access to the old fuel room. Bring what you need to conclude your study.

In God's work we shine the light of glory,
Father Lavasseur

Bernie closed his laptop and placed it on the nightstand. They gave each other a smile and a peck on the lips.

"Good morning," Bernie whispered and saw worry lines in Lilly's forehead.

"Are we really going to go through with this, Bernie?"

"I don't know, are we? I'm not as worried about smuggling the box out of the cathedral, that might be the easy part. I'm concerned about customs."

"I know," Lilly said. "We've had bad luck. I'm tired of sitting in back offices getting peppered with questions."

"If they find the metal, we can't exactly say it's a cordless curling iron," Bernie quipped, then he snuck under the covers and started nibbling.

At work later that morning, Bernie explained to the crew why they would soon manage the store once again. At his silo office, he arranged three days in Albi with flights booked three weeks out. He emailed Father Lavasseur and Attuchi to fill them in on respective details. Attuchi, although discouraged about the lack of new clues, replied with an agreement to fund another trip to look under the work bench.

Chapter 23

Rome, Italy

In the fireplace, charred embers from a distant warmth nestled dark into the log rack as if hiding from a spark. Cardinal Beufort sat with Attorney Tubero discussing the Putnam and Horn case when their canonist knocked, opened the office door and took a couple steps in, said, "Pardon the intrusion, but I have urgent news."

Cardinal Beufort said. "And what have you, then?"

"Bernard Maynard and Lilly Halpers have flights booked for Albi, France."

Beufort and Tubero exchanged knowing looks. Beufort asked, "Why are they going back?"

Tubero replied, "They spent considerable time in a small basement room, so our regents picked the locks and got down there. They found brushed off stones revealing crude chiseled images of animals. There's a work bench along the back wall, a set of empty shelves, and a lawn mower frame. But that's it."

"Right," Beufort said. "So, these images didn't lead them to their next destination as usual. I wonder why not?"

Tubero replied, "Maybe they missed something and need another look."

"That's possible. Try and get someone down there again if they return to that same room."

"I'll get things lined up."

Chapter 24

Albi, France

The flight got bumpy over the eastern Atlantic, but the pilot nailed the landing in Paris, and after a three-hour layover, the connection to Albi went smoothly. They got a rental and drove to an Airbnb near the cathedral, then drove to a grocery store, a hardware store, and a thrift store for supplies.

"I think we have a tan BMW following us," Bernie said on their way back to the Airbnb. He took a sudden right turn and accelerated. Lilly grabbed the ceiling handle and braced with the turn.

"Did he turn with us?"

"He did. Hang on." Bernie made a sudden left turn and checked his mirror.

"And?"

"He went straight, so maybe a coincidence."

"Or they knew we made them."

That night, Bernie and Lilly made spaghetti, then watched a movie. Bernie struggled to concentrate on the plot. Every ten minutes he got up and roamed, checking doors, and peeked out the windows. Just before bed, they double checked their gear laid out ready to load into back packs: transfer paper, charcoal pencils, water, knee pads, hand-held mirror, battery-operated LED lantern, gloves, whisk brooms, screwdriver, hand-held shovel, small tarp, small bath towel, pack of moist towelettes, and to fill the void, one metal cookie box with a paperback book of Douglas Adam's, *The Hitchhiker's Guide to the Galaxy* inside it. The lid fit snuggly on top.

The following morning, meetings kept Father Lavasseur busy until ten, the earliest he could meet Bernie and Lilly. The priest looked good standing near the front alter. *Maybe less stress with monsignor crab-ass gone for a while*, Lilly thought.

"Welcome back my friends," Father Levasseur said with genuine warmth in his tone and opened his arms wide, spreading his white robe like the wings of an angel. "I trust your travels have gone well?"

They shook hands as Bernie replied, "Yes, a little turbulence over the Atlantic rattled our nerves, but here we are safe and sound."

"A true blessing and marvel with our modern flight, and of course thankful there were no great balls of fire," Father Lavasseur said with a sly grin on this face. "By the way, I deeply enjoyed your scriptural references to the carved images. That was a graceful touch."

"We enjoyed looking them up," Lilly replied.

"And as I mentioned," Bernie added, "There might be more images under the work bench. We brought better lighting and other supplies in back packs that are out in the car."

"We're ready to do some more dusty exploring," Lilly said, flashing her charming smile.

Father Lavasseur read their body language and the couple seemed fully at ease, he said, "Well, fantastic. I look forward to what new carvings will be brought to light."

"How is Monsignor Dubaux doing?" Lilly asked.

Father Lavasseur replied, "He's okay, but there's some question if he will be able to return, as least not at his former capacity."

Lilly watched the corners of the father's lips curl up slightly and heard a meliorative tone in his voice as he continued, "At times he can seem a bit gruff, but he is a good man and I pray for him that he may have a quick recovery."

"Indeed," Bernie said. "We appreciate you for allowing us to explore this small bit of history."

"The history of the fuel room," Father Lavasseur replied, then asked, "Is that what you will call your book, Lilly? I mean if you proceed with one."

Lilly smiled and said, "Well it's a strong possibility."

"Good, good," the father said as he handed the fuel room key to Bernie. "God showed you a keyhole for knowledge and history, which brought you here, and now, I give you the physical key to our dusty basement. Without further ado, I'll let you two get started."

"You're not coming out with us?" Bernie asked. "I mean, at least out to the door."

"I don't see a need. I went down there after your last visit and looked around. I am intrigued with what you found and see value in your work. You two, go ahead, I trust you." Lilly looked quickly at the floor. Father Lavasseur thought, *There it is again, she's hiding something.*

Bernie and Lilly retrieved their gear from the car, then walked along the cathedral's towering walls to the iron clad door, which unlocked easily and swung open. Bernie riffled through his backpack and took out the lantern. He flipped it on, and the pair descended the stairs. The light above the work bench sputtered to life and added a few paltry lumens to the small piles of dirt dotting the floor, their rounded shadows looked like dunes on a lunar surface.

"Okay, let's get started," Bernie said as he retrieved his whisk broom and swept off the workbench. "We forgot a dustpan."

"Just sweep it to one side."

With that task accomplished, they unpacked the rest of the gear. Bernie spread the tarp on the floor next to the sun stone, strapped on knee pads, and got to work. Using the screwdriver as a lever, he lifted the two target stones and set them aside. Lilly helped scoop out dirt until the box came into view.

Lilly got up and checked the stairs, said, "All clear."

Bernie pulled up the disintegrating box and quickly wrapped it in a small towel, then placed it in his backpack. He retrieved the new metal box with the book inside, and placed it in the hole, then refilled the dirt, tamped it down, and put the stones back in place. He filled in the cracks and gave the area a light coating of fine dirt, then brushed off the middle sections to make it blend in with the rest. He asked, "How does it look?

"Looks like the rest, good job."

"Okay, next project."

With good lighting from the lantern, and protection from the tarp, Bernie laid on his stomach to reach under the workbench's lower shelf. He painstakingly swept off the remaining stones, then, using a mirror, snapped pictures of the four new images. Lilly sketched in her notebook and added the placement of a ram, flower, tree, and a basket to the diagram.

Bernie stood up, took off his knee pads and stretched his back, said with a moan, "Time for a break."

They went outside and cleaned their hands and face with moist towelettes.

After a long pull of water, Lilly said, "We're making good progress." She checked her phone. "We've been at for about an hour and a half."

"We probably have an hour of work left," Bernie predicted.

Two joggers ran by. A man and women who appeared in their mid-thirties slowed, then circled back and struck up a conversation. The man asked something in French.

"We speak English," Bernie said.

"Ah, are you Americans?" the woman asked with a slight accent.

"Yes."

"What brings you to Albi?" the man asked.

"We're historians," Bernie replied. "Doing research on the cathedral."

"Ah," the man replied, then pointed to the open door, asked, "What's going on in the basement, there? Are you looking for something?"

Bernie hesitated, glanced at Lilly, then replied, "The lower room is part of the original structure dating back to twelve eighty-two. It's only part of our research to possibly write a book about the entire cathedral's history."

"Wow, how interesting," the woman said as she advanced toward the open door. "Do you mind if we take a look down there?" Bernie took a couple side steps to block her entrance, almost colliding with her, he said, "You would need to get permission from Father Lavasseur. He's inside if you'd like to go ask." The woman's face was inches from Bernie's and her breath smelled like salami.

"It's quite alright," the woman replied.

"Come let's go," the man said.

"Just curious," the woman said as she backed away, and the pair jogged off.

"She seemed overly pushy," Bernie said.

"They both seemed suspicious," Lilly replied. "Why would she want to go down there so urgently?"

"I bet Beufort was up to that little charade."

"I'll bet your right."

After a few more breaths of fresh air, they returned to the coal room and used tracing paper with large charcoal pencils to make crude replicas of each image. Bernie found it difficult to get good images of the stones under the shelf without ripping the delicate paper, and had to redo a few, but he finally got four acceptable images.

They decided to flatten out the dirt piles using the whisk brooms, recreating a smoother, yet disturbed looking surface throughout the room.

"It looks a little closer to how we found it," Bernie said.

They packed up the gear. Bernie turned off the lantern and put it in his backpack, leaving only the paltry shop light to guide them out.

"Let's call that good," Bernie said, then looked sharply at Lilly. "Last chance to put it all back before we're possible felons."

"No way, Bern, Moridorno would be disappointed in us."

"For stealing?"

"Well, no, because we're taking something no one else alive knows exists and it could benefit future generations."

"That sums it up nicely," Bernie replied as he took one last look around, clicked off the workbench light and they headed up the stairs.

After a short wait near the front altar, Father Lavasseur emerged from the side door, he thanked his cleric, then smiled warmly at the couple, said, "You don't look as dusty this time."

"We were smart enough to bring a tarp and towelettes this time," Bernie replied chuckling and patted his stuffed backpack. He dug in his pants pocket for the coal room key, then handed it to the father. "Before I forget."

"Well, how did you two do? Any new images?" Father Lavasseur asked as he wound the key back on with the rest of his many.

Lilly replied, "As Bernie predicted, we discovered four more images under the workbench."

"Oh?"

"Yes," Lilly continued. "We found a ram, a flower, a tree, and what looks like a basket."

"How wonderful, and if I may, I'd like to add a couple verses right now that readily come to mind."

"Please do," Lilly replied enthusiastically.

"Okay, this one is from Psalms, He will be like a tree firmly planted by streams of water which yields its fruit in its season, and its leaf does not wither; and in whatever He does, He prospers."

"That sounds magical," Lilly said. "And the other?"

"This is an analogy about the basket that applies to everyone. It's from Deuteronomy, that you shall take some of the first of all the produce of the ground which you bring in from your land that the Lord your God gives you, and you shall put it in a basket and go to the place where the Lord your God chooses to establish His name."

Bernie said, "Thank you for the wonderful verses, father. That last one is inspirational in an evangelical sense."

"They all are, really," the father replied. "But that is one of my favorites. I'll email you the passages for your book. Say, are you two still planning to be my guests at mass tomorrow?"

Bernie and Lilly looked at one another to see who would talk first. Lilly smiled and replied, "Yes, we're looking forward to it."

"We'll be at the eight o'clock mass," Bernie added. "We planned this trip to be here on a Sunday so we could see you in action, so, yep, we'll be there." Bernie chuckled, but it sounded forced.

Father Lavasseur looked hard at Bernie, then at Lilly. Something felt off kilter with the young couple. *They seem nervous*, he thought, then replied, "How wonderful. I think you will enjoy it, especially the three readings and a psalm. I will look your way while I read them. They can apply to you."

"We look forward to it," Bernie replied, but made it sound a little bit like a question.

Back at their Airbnb, Bernie and Lilly unloaded the backpacks. Lilly used the remaining towelettes to wipe dust from the gear, then packed most of it in a box destined for local donation.

"We haven't bought any souvenirs yet," Lilly said.

"That's okay," Bernie replied. "Let's consider this more of a business trip, besides, I need that spare room in my suitcase for the metal. Speaking of which, we might as well open the box."

"Pandora's?" Lilly asked sarcastically.

"Maybe." At the kitchen table, Bernie pried open the lid causing rust flakes to scatter on the surface. He said, "This box is shot. I don't think we can keep it."

"Yeah, that's too bad."

Bernie removed the books and warm metal and took the busted-up box out back to the trash bin, a bit of a travesty, but the rust had taken its toll.

Back inside and wearing gloves, they examined the thermal metal, and carefully paged through the books. After temporarily satisfying their curiosity, Bernie wrapped the wool padding around the metal and secured it in a medium sized plastic

Tupperware container, then stuffed the wad in a reusable Aldi's grocery bag and folded over the top. They decided to smuggle the items separately, thinking if the metal got confiscated at customs, the books shouldn't attract attention. As Lilly packed the two books in her suitcase, Bernie nestled the Aldi's bag among his shirts in the middle of his suitcase. That night, sleep teetered on the edge of consciousness as the couple woke at the slightest noise.

The next morning, they loaded the car like trained band roadies. After a short drive to the cathedral, Bernie found a parking spot near the front and in direct sight of the church's surveillance cameras.

As they walked into the cathedral, Bernie said, "Let's drive straight to the airport after mass. Our plane leaves at four-thirty, so we can make sure we get through customs, then hang out, get some lunch at a food court, and maybe walk around for a while."

"Sounds fine with me," Lilly replied. "I didn't want to go back to the Airbnb, it probably got searched and trashed after we left this morning."

"I wouldn't doubt it."

Both raised protestant, Bernie and Lilly found the mass long, but impressively structured. During the reading of scripture, as promised, Father Lavasseur referred to their visit in Hebrews, 13:2, as he read from the pulpit, "Do not forget to show hospitality to strangers, for by so doing some people have shown hospitality to angels without knowing it." Next, he referred to the images in the coal room from Genesis, "Then God said, let us make mankind in our image, in our likeness, so that they may rule over the fish in the sea and birds in the sky, over the livestock and all the wild animals, and over all the creatures that move along the ground."

He looked their way often as he spoke. After the service, Bernie and Lilly waited for the crowd to thin, then chatted briefly with Father Lavasseur before they said good-bye. Bernie promised an email with a revised layout including the new images. Father

Lavasseur promised Lilly an email containing anything more he could discover about the coal room's history.

At the airport, Bernie entered the queue line at customs with his passport in hand. He tried to act casual, but worried that made him look even more suspicious.

"Next."

Bernie stepped up and slid his passport under the plexiglass.

"Anything to claim?" The customs agent asked in a heavy French accent, as he paged through Bernie's passport.

"No."

"Purpose for your time in France?"

"Ah, visiting a friend and we attended a church service which he presided over."

The older male agent looked up and studied Bernie's face through the plexiglass for a few seconds, then took a hard look at his passport photo. The agent tapped on his keyboard and studied his screen.

Behind the booth, off to the right, Bernie felt a little queasy as he watched his suitcase disappear into the scanner. He studied the stoic facial expressions of the middle-aged woman who peered into her screen. She said something to a young female agent as his suitcase emerged and traveled down the conveyer. The young agent moved it to a table and opened it, moved a few articles of clothing around, and ignored the Aldi's bag. The young woman said something to the screen attendant, then zipped up the suitcase and wrapped a green tag around its handle. Bernie breathed a sigh of relief which made the man in the booth look up. He gave Bernie another long stare, then stamped his passport, said, "Have a nice trip."

Lilly had breezed through customs and watched Bernie squirm while he and his possessions got scrutinized. She gave him a peck on the cheek, said, "So far, so good, eh?"

"Looks like we made it."

"Isn't that an old Barry Manilow song?"

Chapter 25

Huntington, West Virginia

Bernie and Lilly felt a wave of relief when they got to their condo safely. Bernie thought a white SUV tailed them for a few turns and set their nerves on fire, but the car backed off and turned. Bernie stashed the Aldi's bag on the floor in their master bedroom closet as they unpacked.

"Remember," Bernie said, "We can't mention anything about what we have until I meet with Sean, not even our parents or employees."

"Oh, I remember. My lips are sealed."

Later that evening, with Bernie's help, Lilly added the new images found under the workbench to the grid and emailed the updated diagram to Father Lavasseur, promising to add the last two biblical passages when things settled down at work. Bernie sent the diagram to Attuchi and Associates and explained without really lying that the four new images did not reveal any new clues.

The next morning, Bernie attended two estate sales, then priced antiques with Lilly after lunch. Just before three, he got a call from Shandra, who had the day off, and fell that morning during a climb with her boyfriend, Chuck.

Lilly noticed Bernie's concerned look and vocal tone. She walked over to his workstation, asked, "What happened?"

Bernie put his phone on speaker as Shandra explained, "Oh my God, it was awful. I lost a foot hold and poor gallant Chuck, he saved us, really. He saw me slip, so got in the hammer position with the catch rope, but an anchor pulled out and that caused a chain reaction, and we popped a bunch on the way down. Luckily, we were only about thirty feet up when the shit show happened, or I might not be talking to you right now. Anyhow, I cracked my ulna. Chuck broke his radius. I'll be in a cast for four months and need about a week off, then the doctor says I should only work half days and ease back into things."

"Sure, of course," Bernie said. "Take as much time as you need."

"Is there anything we can do?" Lilly asked. "Are you still at the ER?"

"No, I'm at my parent's house now and they're taking good care of me."

After the call, Bernie and Lilly sent her texts with funny get-well GIFs and an e-card for food delivery.

Bernie said to Lilly, "You'll have to work out front more often."

"I don't mind. I like waiting on customers. Sorting totes can get a bit monotonous."

"Even when you know there are three more Brandt figurines out there somewhere worth an estimated two point four million?"

"Well, there's always that, but still, it gets tedious at times."

Bernie looked a little hurt.

Early the next morning, Lilly's sister, Beth, called sounding desperate after a rough and premature delivery of a baby girl during the night. She needed to stay in the hospital a few days and hated to ask for help, but with their parents vacationing in Spain, she needed help at home with her two-year old son.

"I just need someone to babysit until me and the baby get released from the hospital, or mom and dad get back from their trip. John needs to work and..."

"I'm on my way," Lilly said.

Bernie watched Lilly pack and gave her words of encouragement, then drove her to the airport to catch her flight to Tulsa. After a long kiss goodbye, Bernie drove to his bank on the way home, and rented the largest sized safety deposit box and, still in the Aldi's bag, locked up the metal for safe keeping.

Back at the condo, he kept their newly acquired books where Lilly left them, hiding in plain sight on their bookshelf, blending in with the multitude of others. Just before bed that night, Bernie paged through the botanical book and tried to match the exotic looking plants with any on the internet; then stared blankly at the strange cryptography until his eyelids felt heavy. He texted Lilly heart emojis and went to bed.

A new routine started at the store during the following week. With Shandra's absence, Bernie gave Seth and Katy keys and the combination to the safe, then taught them how to open. This allowed Bernie time to attend a few estate sales and work in the back room. Four days later, Lilly's mom and dad flew into Tulsa from Spain, the soonest the airlines could arrange. They gladly took over their grandson's care. Lilly stayed an extra day to catch up with family, then she flew home.

Monday morning, Bernie and Lilly stopped by the silo office, lattes in hand. The store slowly resumed its normal hum with Shandra due back at noon to start working half days. A welcome home banner hung over the cash register, with paper plates, plastic forks, party hats and paper blow-outs on the counter next to the cake.

"Well, Bernie, last night you said you wanted to sleep on it, before deciding. You have officially slept on it." Lilly sipped from the hole in her plastic lid.

"I have indeed slept on it and feel pretty good. I think we should proceed with our plan."

"You're sure we can trust Sean and his associate at the university?"

"Sean said David's a good guy, a metallurgist willing to take a look and keep his mouth shut."

That afternoon, Bernie dropped by Sean's office holding the Aldi's bag by the straps like just coming from the market instead of the bank. He knocked on Sean's open office door.

Sean looked up from his desk, said, "Hey Bernie, how's it going my friend? Come on in." Bernie entered the office and put down the bag as Sean stepped out around his desk. They shook hands and gave each other a side hug.

"Please, sit down, gosh, it's good to see you. Can I get you something to drink? I have a stocked mini fridge here."

"No, thanks, I'm good. But next time we meet, let's be drinking a beer."

"For sure, so that must be it, huh?" Sean said, pointing at the bag as he sat back down.

"It is," Bernie replied and placed the bag on the floor next to Sean's desk, then sat down.

"Okay, I'll get it over to David's office before I leave today, he has access to a spectrometer and maybe some other fun scientific toys. I'll let you know when he completes the tests."

"Awesome, I sure appreciate your help. How's work?"

"Good. I'm teaching three courses this semester and working on a new book that examines descendants of families disrupted by the civil war."

"Wow, that sounds intriguing."

"It is, and what I like best is exposing the ripple effect that courses through our lives as time goes on. Like this one man, Everett Nichols, a farmer, married, three young kids, he comes back from the war missing his left leg and right arm, and can't run equipment. The family eventually loses everything they worked so hard for, but simultaneously, he helped save the union. I'm working with a couple of his adult great-grandchildren to fit all the bits and pieces of their life's history together, figuring out who did what. It's like sewing together the fabric of time."

"That sounds really cool, Sean. I love personal touches like that. Let me know when it's out on Kindle."

"I will. I'm getting close."

"So, concerning what's in the bag," Bernie said, lowering his voice. "This needs to stay completely confidential."

"You know you can trust me and David's solid," Sean replied confidently, then smiled at his friend. "I still don't know how you do it. You're like a magnet for weird once in a lifetime finds, and here you go again. What's this one worth?"

"I have no idea, and this time it's not mine. We patched together some logic and followed clues from the Moridorno letter. Your email helped."

Sean looked startled, said, "I didn't think I found anything that important."

"You got us looking in the right direction. We've been traveling a lot chasing leads."

"As I recall, the letter was vague."

"Lilly is a genius when it comes to research, she's relentless. But we did encounter resistance from some Catholic Church folks who used to own the letter. They made minor threats and like to trash hotel rooms. They left us a dead bird."

Sean looked stunned, asked, "Bernie, are you getting me into something dangerous?"

Bernie squirmed in his chair, replied, "Probably, and I don't mean by the potential radiation. I'm kidding, there isn't any, well, that we know of, but that's why I'm here."

Sean's expression continued to sour, he said, "Okay, I don't want to know anything else. I'll take it over to David's office right away, tell him nothing of what you just told me, and yeah, we better keep our mouths shut."

"Good, thank you Sean. I believe this cause will be worth our effort. It's fascinating, feel it. It stays warm."

Sean leaned down and hesitantly tapped the outside of the bag with the back of his hand, then left it in place, said, "Feels like you have a casserole in there."

Bernie smiled, said, "It's in a plastic container, but I wouldn't eat it. Hey, you know I wouldn't normally pull you into something like this, but you have the best access to find out what the hell we have there."

"It's all good, Bernie. We have a passion for history. Why not mix in a little weird science like warm metal in an Aldi's bag."

"Trust me, Lilly and I had a hard time deciding if we should just walk away from this one, but realized we stumbled into an obligation."

On Wednesday midmorning, Bernie received a text from Sean:
Hey, ready to meet with David
How about tomorrow night

Druckers on Uclid? 7 pm
After checking with Lilly, Bernie replied:
  We'll be there.
  Thx

The next night, Bernie, Lilly, Sean, and David walked to a secluded booth toward the back of the hot-wings joint. David carried a manila folder tucked under an arm and the familiar Aldi's bag hung from his fingers. Introductions were exchanged as they sat down and ordered a round of beers. David mentioned he home brewed, so they chatted about the variations in hops and barley until their liquified hops and barley arrived.

Sean took a sip, said, "Cheers, everyone."

Glasses clinked.

"Okay, David," Sean resumed, "Thanks for doing this."

"Not a problem," David replied, then gave a quick look at each person seated at the table. "I can't believe I'm able to be a part of it."

David handed the grocery bag to Bernie who leaned it against his bar stool. David placed the folder on the table and tapped on it, then said, "I have the results here. First off, the Geiger test was negative, and thankfully I found no other eminent hazards." Nods of approval rounded the table.

David added, "Although, I should disclose that under normal circumstances, these compounds would emit high volitivity."

"Does that mean what I think it does?" Bernie asked.

"Yes, only probably worse than you can imagine. It should blow up several square miles and scatter deadly radiation across several states. This metal makes no sense. I'm still nervous being anywhere near it, but I'd rather go quickly here than have my skin peel away slowly in Kentucky."

A hush fell across the table with furtive glances all around. After a few unsettled moments, David continued, "What you have is called a transition metal, it's when a new element is created." He opened the folder, licked a finger, and pulled out a page with a bar graph that showed a high spike followed by many smaller spikes with names listed underneath each one. "As you can see by this spike, almost eighty percent is made with this one component, and it's an unknown element. It shouldn't exist. It doesn't exist, but you have some in your bag there, so it does now, I guess." He paused for effect.

Bernie's eyebrow shot up as he looked around at concerned expressions. Lilly tapped a finger on her lower lip. Sean drained his beer and looked for their server. David continued, "The rest of the components listed are lesser amounts of iridium, rhenium, palladium, and osmium, all known materials with high densities, melting points, and abilities to withstand corrosion. The unknown element by itself is a massive discovery on several levels, but to have this combination remain stable and apparently safe, well, it's off the charts. I can only assume this was made recently?" David looked from Bernie to Lilly to Sean, then back to Bernie. Bernie, Sean, and Lilly glanced at each other with small smiles, then everyone's gaze landed on Bernie. With a lowered voice, he said, "These are details that can't leave this table."

More nods all around. David replied, "Yes, of course."

Bernie said quietly, "Based on evidence during our research, we estimate the metal is at least a thousand years old."

David looked like he bit into a lemon, said incredulously, "You've got to be shitting me. That's impossible. First, they obviously didn't have the technology for this advanced metallurgy, and second, its condition looks too good except for the damaged edges. I should have had it carbon dated that way..."

"Wait," Bernie interrupted. "Right now, its age is irrelevant, so let's move on. What else do you have in your folder there?"

David sat back and gulped some beer. "Oh boy do I ever," he responded like an excited child and pulled out the remaining data from the folder. He licked a finger and looked through the pages, cleared his throat and said, "Okay, here we go. This is a ton of science, so stop me if you have questions. First off, whoever created that metal must have used a particle accelerator to restructure the molecular sequence. Basically speaking, new isotopes were made by removing neutrons from the nuclei, but the proton count remains the same. These share chemical similarities, but the relative atomic mass differs causing perpetual molecular covalent vortices." He licked his thumb and flipped to the next page, looked around at the blank stares, then continued, "Okay, simplified, the unknown element has 123 protons with only 122 electrons, so it's perpetually hungry to add an electron. Then, it's mixed with these other elements causing even more turbidity with billions of small wars going on at the molecular level, microcosmic battles to gain stability, but they never will because of the missing electron. Collectively, this produces the constant thermodynamic energy output of eighty-two degrees Fahrenheit."

"So you have access to this perpetual energy now?" Bernie asked eagerly.

"No," David said flatly, then took a swig of beer. "First, we need to figure out what the unknown element is, then create a formula to keep everything stable, like a recipe to bake pie where the ingredients are listed in specific measurements. With all these variables, I would need access to a supercomputer. And usually, finds like this are shared with other brilliant minds for a collaborative effort."

"Thank you for your discretion in not telling anyone about it," Lilly said, then asked, "What do you think is the most unique feature?"

"What really fascinates me is how they, whoever they are, unbalanced the molecular structure and yet maintain stability. That's the true wonder. Oh, and by the way, this metal is worth a lot of money. For comparison, rhodium is worth fourteen thousand per ounce. Your metal weighs nineteen ounces, so that pencils to at least two-hundred sixty-six K. But its uniqueness and thermal output is obviously priceless. For that reason, I propose you leave the metal at our facility. We have a containment chamber just in case there is some latent danger. Plus, we have the best security measures."

"But how many people will know about it?" Bernie asked.

"Just me and Sean and I had to schedule equipment use with our lab tech, Casandra. She logs everyone's lab time and what piece of very expensive equipment is used, so each department is billed accordingly."

"What did you have to tell her?" Lilly asked.

"Nothing, really. I kept it vague, but all the equipment stores digital results until they are wiped, or cycle through."

"Can you go in and delete that file?" Sean asked.

"No, only Casandra's supervisor, Phil could do that.

"How long does it take to cycle through?" Bernie asked.

"The lab stays busy, so I'd guess about two weeks."

"Crap, I wish I would have known about this," Bernie said.

"Yeah, me, too," Sean added as he looked at Bernie, then at David.

Bernie said, "So that means two more people have access to the report."

"Sorry guys, I should have mentioned that, and no offense, but I get all kinds of quirky requests from people thinking they found something special, like rocks that look like meteorites. I didn't expect the magnitude of what you brought in, Sean. Besides, I doubt Casandra or Phil will open the file, they see dozens of tests come through daily."

Bernie shot Sean a disappointed glance, then replied, "Okay, David, you didn't know. But with that said, I don't think we want to keep the metal at the university."

"I understand. But, if I hear a big boom, I'm not going to bother to run."

Nervous laughter bounced around the table.

After coffee and a bagel, Bernie got in his old, but pampered red Beamer his parents had given him for a high school graduation present and headed to the bank. He carried the grocery bag to the safety deposit box area on the bank's lower level like he'd just come from shopping. After stowing the metal, he headed to work, but stopped at a mud hut and got coffees for the crew. Later that afternoon, he checked his email and saw one from Attuchi. He opened it and read,

Hello Bernie,

Just a quick note here to check in about any progress deciphering the images on the etched stones. Thanks again for sending us the diagram. Our client is excited about your new find but is getting anxious. Does anything lead you to another destination yet?
Best Regards,
Ricardo Attuchi, esq.

Bernie sent back a vague reply about continued research and attached the associated biblical verses hoping to pacify him for a while longer.

The following Monday afternoon, an upset Sean stopped by the store and made small talk with Lilly in the back room while they waited for Bernie to return from a sale.

"He said he would be back by three, something must be holding him up," Lilly said, shrugging her shoulders and looking at her phone. "You can't tell me what this is about?"

Sean looked morose and paced nervously like a caged animal. "I'd rather wait and tell you both."

Ten long minutes later, the bay door opened, and Bernie pulled in with his van. With a concerned look, he got out, asked, "Hey Sean, what brings you to the store?"

"We need to talk. Do you have somewhere private?"

The three walked quickly into the break room; Bernie closed the door, and they sat down. Tension seemed to ooze from Sean's pores.

"Well let's get this elephant out of the room," Bernie said. "What's going on, Sean?"

"There's no way to put this delicately. Casandra, the lab tech, was found dead at her apartment earlier this afternoon."

Lilly gasped. Bernie said, "Oh my god, what happened?"

"It appears she was strangled."

"Oh my gosh, do you think it could be associated with David's report?" Lilly asked.

"I don't know many details. She didn't show up for work this morning and her supervisor couldn't get a hold of her, so he called her mom, who went over and found her. She recently broke up with her boyfriend. They're trying to locate him as a person of interest."

"How awful," Lilly said as she and Bernie exchanged looks and silently shared the question: *Did Beufort and his goons kill someone again?*

Chapter 26

Phil and Casandra

In October around Halloween, Phil Thantos, Casandra's boss, awkwardly joked he didn't need to dress up because he already looked like a nerd. Every day, he wore black, heavy-framed glasses and had his plastic pocket pen protector inserted in his white button-down shirt. Although intelligent, his social skills lacked emotional maturity, proven many times by his failed flirtatious attempts with Cassandra. *Creeped out is a better description,* she often thought.

Phil lived alone, mostly in the basement of his late parents' house gambling online and thinking about Casandra. Obsession can be dangerous and comes in many colors. Delusion blends them all into a dull grey. Phil liked Texas Hold 'Em the best, and some nights played into the wee hours. After weeks of bad luck, he woke up one morning owing one hundred seventy thousand dollars to fourteen short term, high interest credit card lenders. *I just need one lucky night.* Eventually, Phil's car got repossessed, so he rode the bus to work, making him feel humiliated sitting with all the low-lifes. He dreamed of hitting a progressive jackpot on a maximum bet. *It's okay, I can win it all back. I just need a little more seed money, then I'll take Casandra out in my new Ferrari Sf90 Stradale.* Phil looked out the bus windows at the downtown buildings that seemed to fly past him and blurred everything into a dull grey.

Not much got by Phil at work, so when the unusual spectrograph came through, he opened it immediately and saw dollar signs. After making a few calls, Phil arranged a deal worth two hundred dollars for a copy of the unique report. On the designated day, he clicked on copy and paste, then while waiting for the download, gawked out his office window at Casandra, who sat at her desk working on her computer. *She looks like a doll,* he thought.

The small record icon lit up on Casandra's task bar. Wondering why, she glanced in at Phil, who made eye contact. He looked surprised, then guilty. Both looked away quickly. Casandra took a sip from her coffee cup, then opened a desk drawer and pretended to look for something.

Shit, she knows I'm copying something again, Phil thought as he left his office, and walked over to Cassandra. Worried she'd squeal, he asked, "You saw that, didn't you?"

"I noticed you must have recorded something if that's what you mean. Why are you acting so weird, Phil? I don't know what it was, and I don't care anymore." Casandra slumped her shoulders and stared at her computer screen. Phil hovered a few uncomfortable moments taking labored breaths that rattled his esophagus. He became caught up in dark thoughts. *I hate her insolent tone and lack of respect, but she's so pretty and smells like honey.* Then, as if emerging from a stupor, Phil turned around and returned to his office, checked his Venmo account, then forwarded the file to his buyer. He sat at his desk and leered at Cassandra, upset with her constant rejections and lack of respect and now she could get him fired.

At home on Sunday, Cassandra put her lunch plate in the kitchen sink when she heard the doorbell. Looking through a window, she saw Phil standing on her front porch. Wearing a ball cap, sunglasses, polyester brown pants and Velcroed sneakers, he rocked back and forth with his hands stuffed in his jacket pockets. She shook her head and opened the door a crack, just enough to peak out and speak. "Hi Phil, what's going on? What do you want?"

"Yes, hello Casandra, well I can't help thinking about the file I copied. I may have done something and feel badly. Can we talk about it? I'll be gone in a couple minutes."

Cassandra rolled her eyes, thought a moment, and asked, "Can't this wait until tomorrow, Phil? It's my day off, go home." She closed the door but could hear Phil as he raised his voice. "I know, I know, and I'm sorry, but I can't sleep, and I'd like to get something off my chest. Just a quick minute and I'll be gone."

She cracked open the door and studied Phil for a few seconds. He smiled pathetically.

She rolled her eyes, unlatched the safety chain, and let him in, but picked up her phone from the end table.

"You have two minutes," she said, and motioned for Phil to sit down in a chair near the window.

That's when she noticed the blue latex gloves.

After a few moments of extreme discomfort, tears wet the rims of Phil's eyes as he hugged Cassandra's cooling body lying on the carpet.

"I'm sorry," he whispered. "You know I'll always love you."

Police would later find Cassandra's phone under her body with a nine and a one entered on the keypad.

With his hands back in his pockets, Phil walked casually to his car, parked down the street, to retrieve a small brown bag with items collected premeditatively from two bars a few blocks from Cassandra's apartment. He returned to the scene of his crime, and spread room by room a buffet of DNA, including three cigarette butts from different ash trays, several used paper towels from restroom trash cans, two random beer bottles taken from a recycling bin in an alley; he unrolled a baggie and used tweezers to pluck pubic hairs gleaned from the rims of different urinals and a woman's toilet. He had enough to plant a curly gem in every room, then he placed his favorite item on Cassandra's nightstand: freshly chewed gum unstuck from under a bar table. *That ought to keep forensics busy for a while.*

Chapter 27

The Magazine Reporter

The buyer of the metals file, a midlevel reporter for Scientific America Magazine with the by line, Dirk Meadows, made the front cover with his outlandish story about stable nuclear material that emits heat. His article caused a loud buzz among the science world, clanking might be a better description, mostly criticism. Dirk fielded many calls, from scientists to garage hobbyists, but his editor made him promptly return a call from The Office of Occupational Safety and Health Administration. Officer, Pamela Jenkins, a specialist in hazardous waste, asked Dirk for the source of his story since it mentioned radioactive materials, although her tone sounded skeptical. Pamela held a PHD in Chemistry from Harvard and knew her stuff. She read the article, but figured the case was another wild goose chase. *Wasn't possible,* she reasoned. Phil made no conditions about confidentiality, so Dirk told her where to find him.

Pamela looked online for the location of Phil's office at the university, then cold-called him at the metals lab. Surprised by the unscheduled visit, Phil put down his hotdog, stood up from his desk as bun crumbs tumbled down his half-tucked shirt. He invited her in.

"Have a seat," he said, sounding annoyed, and motioned to the chairs in front of his desk.

"Thank you. I'll only take a minute of your time. I'm Pamela Jenkins from the Office of Occupational Safety and Health Administration."

Phil said, "It's obvious your offices don't communicate. I've already said everything, and I really didn't know her well."

"Know who?"

"Cassandra Clark."

"I don't know who that is, Mr. Thantos. I'm here to inquire the legitimacy of a metallurgy report you sold to a reporter." Pamela pulled a magazine with Dirk's article from her purse, leaned forward, and placed it in on his desk in front of him. "I'm here to find out if you actually tested something that contain these volatile elements along with the unknown one, the eighty percent."

Phil looked mildly relieved as he glanced at the article, then tipped back his chair and replied, "I don't test anything, just manage the equipment and data." He took a bite of hotdog.

Pamela asked incredulously, "So you're telling me this report is real, and someone tested a metal with these properties in your lab here at the university?"

Phil didn't answer right away. He chewed and swallowed, then used a fingernail to dig at a chunk of meat stuck in his teeth.

"Mr. Thantos?"

Phil nibbled on the retrieved chunk, said, "Yes. It was tested here by one of our professors."

"Did you get a look at what was tested?"

"No, I usually just see the data."

Pamela looked shocked as the reality and severity settled in, she said, "You can't be serious. You...we should be dead from radiation. I... I need to report this." She retrieved her phone. "This whole campus could be contaminated. I need to shut it down."

"Wait!" Phil said loudly, "It's safe. You read the article, it lists the negative Geiger results, the dosimeter and radiograph schedules read null. The report is true, it's stable and inert. I'm fine. You're fine. There is zero emittance. Don't ask me how, I only have a master's in chemistry, so this is way above my pay grade."

Pamela shook her head and replied, "This isn't feasible. Any chance your equipment is faulty?"

"Not likely. United Lab Services comes quarterly to calibrate and load certification updates. Plus, most of this equipment has built in diagnostics. If a parameter goes out, the equipment tells us how to fix it, like in this case, wavelength range and spectral balance is working fine."

"Okay, I'm starting to believe you," Pamela said with consternation as she put down her phone. "But this goes against what we know about physical properties, plus we don't know the long-term stability of this thing, so I need the name of the professor who ran these diagnostics. And you're not off the hook, I'm sure the university will be interested to learn you're selling information on the side."

Fight or flight set in as Phil looked from Pamela's eyes to her neck. He dug his fingernails into the foam of his chair's arm rests as he considered unleashing his rage.

Pamela noticed his agitation and dilated pupils and wondered if he was on something. "Mr. Thantos, are you all right?"

Phil replied with urgency, his voice strained, "I think you should leave now."

"Not before I get the name."

Phil stayed quiet and looked perturbed, glancing from her eyes to her neck, attempting to balance his conflicting emotions.

Pamela eased some of the pressure, said, "I'll tell your superiors you were helpful and cooperative with this case. Now tell me the name."

Phil swiveled his chair and looked out his office window, then said with a sigh, "David Anderson. His office is in the Henderson Engineering Building."

Pamela ran her finger along the posted hours outside David's office, then walked up one flight of stairs. She sat in the hall outside room 208 Henderson Hall and checked her email. Ten minutes later, four tones sounded, and students streamed out of the room. When Pamela entered, David looked up at the black woman standing at the top of the stairs in the large, sloped seating arena. He stopped packing books in his satchel and asked, "Can I help you?"

"Yes, hello, my name is Pamela Jenkins. I'm with OSHA, are you David Anderson?"

"Yes."

"Sir, I need a minute of your time."

Chapter 28

Busted

Pamela looked up when the bells chimed above her as she walked into Bernie's Collectibles. Katy stepped out from the front counter, asked, "Hi, can I help you find anything?"

"Does Bernie or Lilly work here?"

"Yes, they're in the back. Right through there," Katy said, pointing.

"Thank you."

After terse introductions, Bernie led them into the break room and closed the door. Pamela spelled out what she knew, causing dower looks from Bernie and Lilly.

"The metal is in my bank safety deposit box," Bernie confessed right away.

Pamela looked like she swallowed a bug, said, "I should really send a hazmat team and a bomb squad there right now and have you arrested for illegal possession and storage of volatile radioactive materials, possession of a deadly weapon, and suspected terrorism."

Bernie looked sternly, but earnestly at Pamela, said, "We're not terrorists."

"Well, I saw the report and David Anderson told me it's producing heat. That could be a precursor to an explosion. You could be held responsible for hundreds, possibly thousands of deaths if that thing goes off."

"We have reason to believe it's been stable for centuries," Lilly volunteered with a steady tone, trying to defuse the tension.

"You don't know that. How can you know that?"

Lilly explained, "We were hired by an Italian law firm to investigate a letter from the fifteen hundreds. The letter held clues left by its author."

"That's how we found the metal," Bernie added. "Clues from the letter led us to it. We believe a priest named Despachal Moridorno knew about the metal and hid it in fifteen eighty-two."

Pamela cocked her head and asked, "Where did you say you found it?"

"We found it buried in the basement of a church in Europe, but we're not going to give exact details."

"Well, I should get a search warrant for your bank box right now and take you in for questioning, then we'll get the exact details out of you."

"Look, I'll voluntarily turn the metal over to you tomorrow morning so you can do your own tests, but technically, it's not ours, so we're in a bit of pickle. I need to send out some correspondence before any of this hits the press."

"You certainly are in a pickle, and I'm calling the cops right now unless you feed me some details and convince me why I should wait until morning."

"Okay, we found what looks like a broken piece of silver colored metal, about two inches thick and a little bigger than my hand. It looks like it hit something and broke off. It emits a low amount of heat, and all the tests indicate it's stable and has been for centuries. We're betting our lives it will remain so."

Pamela shook her head and dug in her pantsuit pocket for a business card, then laid it on the table. She said, "Here's my card. Your story sounds just crazy-nuts enough for me to believe, but I will get this sorted out. Bring in the metal tomorrow to that address. Get to your bank when it opens and be in my lobby by ten or I'll get search warrants and have you and Lilly arrested."

That night, with Lilly's help and encouragement, Bernie sent out correspondence, some painful to write. First, Bernie opened a blank email message, took a deep breath, and began typing:

Dear Father Lavasseur,

I'm writing this on behalf of myself and Lilly as a confession for not revealing everything we knew about the basement room at Saint Cecelia's. We removed something that was not ours, so I'm going to explain things, and ask for understanding and forgiveness. I'm afraid we've made a mess of things.

We found a small section of unusual metal about the size of a man's hand buried under the stone with the image of the sun (see floor diagram). This metal is unusual because it emits self-producing heat. We discovered it during our first trip but left it there. After a lot of thought and reflection, we retrieved it during our second visit and brought it back to the U.S. for tests. We didn't tell you because we knew you would be obligated to report it, and we felt a connection with Father Moridorno.

We planned to tell only a couple of people at our local university, but unfortunately, a lab worker sold the test results to a reporter. You can see his article about the uniqueness of the metal in the magazine, Scientific America (*I attached photos of the article). Now the whole thing has spiraled out of control and the federal government has the metal for more testing, with no guaranteed return due to the potential danger of radioactive elements.

Tragically, an assistant from the university metal's lab was found murdered at her apartment. We're praying it's not related to the stolen report. I say this because I think you should know, we experienced threats and scare tactics including dead birds and trashed rooms during our travels while we followed Moridorno's clues. Have you ever heard of a Cardinal Beufort and the Successors to the Apostles? We believe he is somehow responsible for these attempts to dissuade our search because the previous owner of the Moridorno letter made public claims about satanism associated with the Catholic Church. The tabloids ran articles about Moridorno, including linking the Catholic Church to a missing Italian hiker, who also happened to be the previous owner of the Moridorno letter. Attuchi's client is his brother, so in effect, we're working for him.

Ultimately, we realized Moridorno wanted someone to find the metal by following his clues. We feel lucky and honored to be the ones to do so, but also feel an obligation to the future of mankind to investigate its potential, especially the unique characteristic for perpetual energy. For these reasons we betrayed your trust and ask forgiveness and will always carry guilt in our hearts. Lastly, we realize you may press charges for our illegal activity, but humbly request your mercy and leniency.

Sincerely,
Bernie Maynard and Lilly Halpers

Lilly read through it one more time, then Bernie pushed send and clicked open a new message and typed:

To: Ricardo Attuchi, and associates

Ricardo,
I have information concerning the Moridorno letter. We discovered an unusual piece of silver metal about two inches thick, slightly larger than a man's hand during our trips to Albi. I say unusual because it emits self-producing heat. It is our opinion, the metal is the target of the clues left in Moridorno's letter, and under our contract, the metal belongs to your client, but there are a few issues to work through. First, we removed it from a private institution without permission and brought it back to the United States. Since it emits heat, we felt obligated to have it tested right away.

We used a metals lab at our local university, and unfortunately, a copied report was leaked to a reporter. You can read the article in this month's Scientific America Magazine. I attached photos of the article which explains what the metal is made of, including stabilized radioactive materials and an unknown element that seems to safely bind it all together. Due to the dangerous components, the US government investigated the story, and demands possession of the metal. I meet with them in the morning (U.S. time) and will tell them about our contract.

One last item, during the testing phase we found out the metal has an estimated monetary value of $266 thousand, U.S. dollars. Although with its unusual characteristics, it's probably worth many times that.

Sincerely,

Bernie Maynard

With Lilly's approval, Bernie pushed send and then opened his Word program since Bernie didn't have Beufort's email address. He typed:

Dear Cardinal Beufort and associates of Successors to the Apostle,

I have a strong hunch your office is responsible for repeated threats, harassment, and vandalism egressed against myself and my research assistant over the past few months, and we hope you are not responsible for Casandra's death. (If you are, you'll know what I mean.)

Just so you know, we did find something profound using clues from the Moridorno letter, a chunk of broken metal that doesn't appear to have been made locally since it produces perpetual heat. So, who knows, maybe it does have something to do with Satan. By the time you read this, the U.S. government will have taken possession of it. So please stop harassing us or I may need to hire Attuchi and Associates to harass you. That might make headlines, too!

Sincerely,

Bernie Maynard

P.S. We don't work for Attuchi anymore and we're not looking for anything, so back off!!!

Bernie folded a printed copy into an envelope addressed to Beufort, sealed it, and handed it to Lilly, he said, "That one felt pretty good to write."

"I'll mail it off tomorrow," Lilly replied.

Coffee in hand and much earlier than necessary, Pamela waited in the lobby of the Department of Labor building with two agents, Detective Wentz from the FBI, and Officer Ducker from the CIA. They all stood slightly apart from each other like repelling magnets and didn't say much. A uniformed police officer stood in the back next to a guy wearing a yellow hazmat suit up to his waist, with the upper section and hood draped over an arm.

At nine forty, Bernie walked into the lobby carrying a bulky Aldi's grocery bag; Lilly followed him.

Pamela and the two agents approached Bernie, she asked him, "Is that it?"

Bernie nodded and held out the bag. "It is."

The guy quickly pulled on the hazmat suit, zipped up, and took the bag from Bernie, then walked quickly out the front door. In the street, a black van pulled up and the side door slid open, revealing two other people wearing hazmat suits. They helped the guy with the Aldi's bag get in, the door slid closed, and the van sped off.

From the lobby Bernie and Lilly followed the legal contingency to an elevator, then up to a conference room on the seventh floor where they answered questions causing a lot of eye rolling. Wentz and Ducker found the story absurd and gave it little credence. Pamela wrapped up the interrogation and the feds decided not to press charges.

"Yet," Ducker said. "We still might if any of this B.S. pans out."

Wentz chimed in, "And keep your mouths shut. No one needs to hear about this."

Wentz and Ducker conversed in the hallway after the meeting, poking mutual fun at the situation.

"Actually," Ducker said, "I could care less if they talk about it. They're probably just looking for publicity or some other angle to make money."

Wentz said, "More frickin' loonies wasting everyone's time."

The following morning, Pamela requested warrants out of an abundance of precaution. That afternoon, the feds searched Bernie's Collectibles while the crew waited on the front sidewalk. Bernie and Lilly's condo received a quick Geiger once through, freaking out the neighbors, then Bernie's bank was evacuated while a hazmat team looked for signs of latent radiation but found nothing unusual. The newspapers and social media caught wind of all the hullabaloo and included pictures of men in orange hazmat suits holding out Geiger wands at the bank.

When questioned by reporters, a trained media specialist explained, "We acted on a tip about suspected illegal weapons. We found nothing and there are no threats to public safety. We now believe the tip was a hoax."

Bernie and Lilly notified their parents to let them know they were fine and in no danger, although there may be pending legal ramifications, and they were in a bit of a pickle. They stopped by the store to calm the raw nerves of their crew.

Except for Seth. "I thought it was awesome," he said calmly.

Lilly stayed in the back room to sort totes, while Bernie walked over to his silo office and called Sean to update him on the situation. Then, Bernie checked his email and got excited when he saw replies from Attuchi and Father Lavasseur.

Bernie called Lilly, who ran over to the silo and stood behind him sounding winded. He clicked one open and they read,

Dear Bernie and Lilly,

My, what a spectacular story you shared and what a crooked web you have spun. I prayed I was wrong when I detected deceit in your body language and odd impressions on the workbench. I'm pleased I still possess that ability to read people but feel remorse with my correctness as my trust in you turned into dust like you collected while digging up my basement. As a representative of Saint Cecelia, I should alert my superiors and the Albi police of your theft and demand the metal's return.

Corinthians says theft causes greed, drunkards, slanderers, and swindlers. Timothy links theft to the love of money. But I can't attach any of these negative labels on the two of you. I sense you are on the side of goodness but have cast our relationship into a dark predicament. I suppose Father Moridorno shares some of the blame, therefore, I find little comfort making any decisions in this regard whatsoever. I have prayed for a resolution that suits best responsibilities for my beloved Saint Cecelia, benevolence, and the two of you. So, I resolve to take a vow of silence concerning what you found. If anyone comes here asking questions or snoops in the basement, I will tell them nothing. And I want nothing more to do with this situation and unfortunately, this includes you and Lilly. Please give her my best, for this will be my last correspondence, and tell her I can no longer provide support for her book. I will only see you again if you ask my help seeking comfort in our Lord.

Go in Peace my friends,
Father Pierre Lavasseur

Bernie felt relieved Father Lavasseur would not press charges, but a knot formed in the back of his throat, knowing he burned a bridge of friendship to a very kind and just man.

"That's too bad," Lilly said. "But I respect his decision."

Bernie nodded, took a drink of water and opened the email from Attuchi:

Hello Bernie,

Our client is excited to hear about what you found, especially its heat producing properties. However, we are disappointed you did not bring the metal directly to us. In effect, you violated your contract, but at this time, we will not pursue damages. I do ask that you waive any future rights to the metal's ownership. We will contact your local OSHA and file an injunction for the metal's return to our client.

Please find two attachments that terminate our contract. E-Sign and return them promptly and send any final restitution requests within seven days. On behalf of Attuchi, Bordino, and Parletto, and our client, we thank you and assistant Halpers for your unbridled persistence and resilience in finding this new treasure.

Best Regards,
Ricardo Attuchi, esq.

Chapter 29

Beufort's Office

With the flue fully open, the fire grew quickly sucking in fresh air causing the fire to roar up the chimney like a fat red dragon. Cardinal Beufort's canonist stood aside after delivering Bernie's letter. Beufort, seated at his desk, tore open the envelope and read Bernie's accusations.

"You may go," Beufort said to his canonist, then picked up his cell phone and called Attorney Tubero.

"Tubero here. Hello Cardinal."

"Scott, I just got a letter from Bernie Maynard."

"Oh?"

"He seems a bit scattered and went on a rant basically accusing us of harassment and knows we're following them."

"Well, he has a point, there," Tubero replied.

"He also claims they found what Moridorno intended them to find."

"Oh? And what is that?"

"He said it's some piece of broken metal that has heat producing properties and the U.S. government planned to confiscate it."

Tubero laughed, said, "That sounds far-fetched, but confirms Moridorno had something worth finding."

"Also, Attuchi is attempting to obtain possession of the metal for his client. What do you suggest we do next?"

"Legally, I see no way to intervene. At some point, I think we should cut our losses and let this case go."

"Drop it completely?" Beufort asked?

"Yes, especially now that Moridorno's clues have been solved, the letter is obsolete."

"That's a good point. Plus, Maynard mentioned something about a dead woman named, Casandra."

Tubero sounded surprised. "What? No, that wasn't us. I have no idea who that is, but another good reason to let this case go."

A silence ensued while Beufort weighed his options.

"Hello, cardinal, are you still there?" Tubero eventually asked.

"Yes, yes. Okay, I agree. Call off the surveillance. I'll have the canonist change the file's classification. We can discuss closure details at next week's meeting."

Chapter 30

A Surprise Party

A week after the federal raid, as the story got named by Seth, the store resumed its traditional hum.

At the condo, working at the kitchen table most evenings, Lilly began to write her book about the Moridorno letter and the hidden clues.

"Still going to call it Bernie's Collectibles?" Bernie asked.

"No, you were right, that title is boring. I've been thinking about some other names, like maybe I'll call it Moridorno's Letter, or, Secrets in the Coal Room, or Aditya's Warm Sun's Rays"

"I like that last one," Bernie quipped.

During the next few days, Lilly and the crew planned a surprise party to be held at the store for Bernie's pending birthday. With all the craziness, Bernie forgot about the red chair with potential Napoleonic ties, but Lilly didn't, and carved out times in the backroom to do clandestine research and decided to reveal the provenance she found as one of his birthday gifts.

She looked online at dozens of photos showing rooms with furniture from various locations Bonaparte lived and finally matched the chair to the Chateau de Fontainebleau, in The Palace of Monarchs. She found identical chairs with the backrest upholstered with red material and embossed gold patterns once used in a Grand Apartment next to the Throne Room. And for added icing on his birthday cake, the chairs had been ordered for a visit from Pope Pius VII. *That ought to get you your usual high dollar provenance, Bern,* Lilly thought as a mischievous grin tickled the corners of her mouth, then she licked the envelope for his birthday card and sealed it with a kiss.

The morning of the big day, Lilly poked her head in the bathroom door and told Bernie she needed to leave the condo early to run a few errands before work. He stopped shaving and said good-bye, then clicked on the electric and dug into his whiskers a bit more aggressively. *She forgot my birthday.*

Instead of running errands, Lilly met the crew, Sean, and Bernie's parents at the store to decorate the back room with streamers, banners and party favors. Other guests arrived and parked a couple blocks away. The cake adorned the center of a workstation. A variety of colorfully wrapped gifts and birthday cards surrounded the cake.

"He's parking his car!" Katy said as she hurried into the back room. Everyone quit talking and stood still. Lilly killed the lights.

At ten to nine, Bernie unlocked the store's front door and stepped in with a concerned look. The lights weren't on. *No one's here yet to open the store?* He checked his phone and saw no messages, then flipped up the bank of light switches for the front of house. With a pissed off demeanor, he walked briskly through the isles into the dark back room and clicked on those lights.

Acknowledgements

Many thanks to the many kind people who so generously contributed in a variety of ways to help form the delivery of this story! To Stephanie Stratton, thank you for being my sounding board, sharing ideas, and books about editing, and for the magazines you brought home from Ned Hickson's editing and writing group. Thank you, Ned, for your suggestions and technical advice.

To my daughter Taryn Yerigan, an aspiring writer with many side interests that keep her life enriched, thank you for the awesome suggestions, editing tips, and available learning tools. Thanks to my big brother, Randy Yerigan, whom I've always looked up to. He was my first victim to read a rough draft and told me most of it sucked, 'but keep the exciting parts'.

Thanks to Randy and Ann Olin, who also read an early version and steered me to logical key transitions in the story. Thank you, Colin Buchanan, for your keen editing skills and staying up so late reading. Thank you, Kathy Skelly, for your suggestions and going through the story with your sharp editor's eye for fine details.

<u>Next in the Series</u>

Bernie's Collectibles

~ The Sakyan Scrolls ~

Bernie and Lilly travel overseas as volunteers to digitize historic relics, some never read in recent times.

Of course, they discover something unique that holds mysteries to unravel. Bernie calls home to say their plans have changed and off they go...Again!

Available Now on Amazon

Made in the USA
Monee, IL
21 October 2024

67726373R00115